Ruby's Imagine

Ruby's Imagine

WRITTEN BY KIM ANTIEAU

Houghton Mifflin Company
Boston 2008

www.houghtonmifflinbooks.com

The text of this book is set in Cochin.

Library of Congress Cataloging-in-Publication Data
Antieau, Kim.
Ruby's imagine / written by Kim Antieau.

p. cm.
Summary: Tells the story of Hurricane Katrina from the point of view of
Ruby, an unusually intuitive girl who lives with her grandmother in
New Orleans but has powerful memories of an earlier life in the swamps.
ISBN 978-0-618-99767-1
[1. Secrets — Fiction. 2. Community life — Louisiana — New Orleans — Fiction.
3. Hurricane Katrina, 2005 — Fiction. 4. New Orleans (La.) — Fiction.] I.
Title.
PZ7.A62987Ru 2008
[Fic] — dc22
2007047736

Manufactured in the United States of America
MP 10 9 8 7 6 5 4 3 2 1

*In memory of my friend
Linda Ann Ford,
who talked to the animals,
birds, bees, and me*

CHAPTER 1

A BUTTERFLY the color of my name did tell me that a Big Spin was coming our way. I was standing by Mr. Grant's wisteria, which hung over his fence and down into our yard, when Ruby Butterfly, this jeweled metamorphosis of a cattypillar, landed on a bright green wisteria leaf like some kind of winged oracle and looked straight at me; we exchanged glances, you know, the way liked-minded and soul-bodied creatures can. We understood each other down deep to our transfigured and transforming cellular parts, and I knew the Big Oaks had told Ruby Butterfly and now she was letting me in on the not-so-secret secret: a storm was coming. Her message was akin to "Run fer ya lives!" in Big Oak and Ruby Butterfly speak. Or, "Stay and watch if you the stomach fer it."

I thanked Ruby Butterfly, who had flown back to the blue, for letting me know, and I watched Samuel Beckett Sparrow hop down from the aboves to my feet. He pecked at the dirt, and I wonders how I could warn the others. No times like this one right now. I went back into the house and to the kitchen, where Mammaloose was cooking red beans and rice. Uncle Gilbert sat at the table reading the papers and stirring his coffee — round and round his spoon went, creating its own little Big Spin.

"Where you been?" Mammaloose asked. "Never seen anyone who took so long gettin' from one place to 'nother like you."

"I stopped at the library with Jacob," I told her. "We have a report due on hurricanes." This was near to the truth.

"Set the table," Mammaloose told me.

She seemed in one of her good-time moods, so I needed to make my words full of care. Mammaloose never hears my words as glad tidings. She says I is constantly putting a target on myself by using my Ruby words.

When I was small Mammaloose could not tolerate my Ruby words at all. Sometimes she whipped me with a leather belt she said my daddy used to hit me with before he died in the car crash with my momma. I knew her words were not part of the true imaginings. My daddy would never have harmed a hair on my head, arms, or legs, and not any other part of my being. Not with purpose. Not like Mammaloose used to do. She doesn't touch me with hurt anymore these years. JayEl—that's what I call Jacob—says it's because I'm bigger than she is now. Maybe she is afraid of you, he says.

No matters.

I pulled plates out from the cupboard and put them on the wooden table. Uncle Gilbert gave me cheerful glances as I set the plate near him. Fork. Knife. Glass. I poured beer in the glasses of Mammaloose and Uncle Gilbert.

"I think a big hurricane is coming our way," I said, likes I was talking about the weather—which I suppose I was.

"I never heard nothing," Mammaloose said.

"Wouldn't matter though. We been through so many storms, so many floods. This house danced with Betsy and came away just fine. And everything since."

Mammaloose says any part of her house stand up to any part of anything else. Except maybe the roof. She be after Uncle Gilbert to fix it since before the last storm ate a piece of it for lunch. She loves this house so much, she says, she chose a man who would fit the house; he had to be small enough for the low ceilings. So, she says, she looks around until she came up short with Uncle Gilbert. He cringe when she puts those kinds of words on him. And then he has another beer. He know how to hide. Same as me. We all have the urges to survive. And I has swamp learning. Knows how to survive and thrive even in the difficulties. Even in the Mammaloose difficulties.

"I ain't worried about no hurricane," Mammaloose said.

Mammaloose and I sat at the table with Uncle Gilbert, who is no uncle to me, and we ate rice, beans, and cornbread, just like we did every Monday. Silence between us. The house sighed, the way houses do when they grow weary of the quiets. Mammaloose stared at her food while she ate. She did not notice me thanking the food for giving up its life for me. After living almost my whole life with Mammaloose, I had learned to say my talks with food and other things in the silence so only the intended of my words could hear.

I have some memories of my before-Mammaloose life, but she says I have lived with her from the minute my parents died when I was five, and before that I lived next door in a little shotgun house. I don't remember living in that house. I do has images in my mind of the swamp and my sisters, Opal and Pearl. I can hear my daddy's voice, see the white alley gator Daddy called his good luck—though I don't see how much good luck that white alley gator could have brought if my daddy got killed in a car crash. I has memories of waking up during a *fais do-do* and some-one shushing me back to sleep while the party went on and on in the other room. I has more images of watching someone make jambalaya—seeing hands chopping vegetables. Hearing singsongs.

Mammaloose says, "That's just Ruby's imagine. She don't know nuthin' about nuthin', especially no swamp. Too many stories from her daddy, that's all."

I do sometimes have wonderings why Mammaloose never talks about my mother—her daughter. She has no photographs of my momma or daddy. Does she have reasoning for this? When I was small I asked. I ask no more.

If I want conversing, I talks with the Flying or Rooted People, or with JayEl. Jacob Lazarus. He has a love for words like I does. Make every sentence a singsong. A *fais do-do*. He understands words have their purposes. They be magic. Conversing is not supposed to be like the white noise music I hears in elevators or at the big box stores. No. Conversing is a hearing, feeling adventure in conjuring, loving, and connecting. JayEl feels the same.

If JayEl not around, I might goes to the Place Where My Vegetables Grow, which is in the back of Mammaloose's house. Or maybe I go to the Crossroads. The first time Uncle Gilbert took me to the

Crossroads, I was just a child. The lady behind the counter gave me a frozen cup. The first taste did tell me it was made of more than ice and syrup.

"*Cher*, you like my sno-ball?" the lady asked.

I nodded.

"It's magic. You never be da same, *cher*. *Laissez les bons temps rouler.*" She winked.

A galaxy did reveal itself to me in her winking eye.

A man be there, too. He shake hands with Uncle Gilbert, who called him Callaway Lanier. They talks about price of something while I looked at the stars in the lady's eye. She smile at me sweetlike.

I didn't go back to the Crossroads till I was about twelve. Went solitaire. Wandered inside and saw the Lady with the Galaxy in Her Eye. She handed me a frozen cup, like before, like this had been a kind of habit thing between us forever, a ceremony. I took it.

"What you need?" she asked me.

"A garden," I says to her. I had tried growing a garden, but nothing come up.

"The whole world can be a garden, dawlin'," she said. "You trying to set down roots? Lessee what I can do."

I followed her to the back of the store, where she did have candles lit and a kind of shrine with flowers and such around the Mary and some of da Saints that I had no recollecting of since Mammaloose made with certainty I never been near a Catlick church. That be Daddy's religion, not Momma's, not Mammaloose's. Mammaloose used to be going to the church of John the Baptist, but no more.

I did have glad feels coming to the back room of the Crossroads with the Lady. A wave of heat touched my skin, as though a hand ran across my cheeks and forehead, like someone blind was figuring out who I was. Alongside those candles and pictures were bottles filled with plants. Maybe other things too. I had not much looking time. The Lady was holding out a few plastic bags. She began dropping seeds into those bags.

"These seeds are beginnings, *cher*," she said. "They be blessed. You remember that."

As we left the back room, I turns around to say my farewell to the whoever's residing there.

"You touched, *cher*?" the Lady asked.

"I have the feels of home back there," I said.

She nodded. "You is home, dawlin'. The whole world is your home."

At the Lady's counter was Mr. Lagniappe, like before. I calls him Mr. Lagniappe now 'cause he brought a little extra into my living, but then he was just Mr. Lanier.

"You planting a garden?" he asked back then. "That a fine thing. I bring you some manure from the zoo, if you like. That help them seeds." He made the glancing eyes at the Lady and I sees then the love going out from him to her. She pay no mind to his glances—or else she had no knowing of their meaning.

The Lady nodded. "He can do right by your garden, *cher*. Even the Earth needs good eats."

The next day, Mr. Lagniappe brought zoo manure to the garden when Mammaloose was at work. And he did so the next year and the next. I never had trouble growing nothing after that. Mammaloose has never had a meeting with the Lady or Mr. Lagniappe, so she has a belief that they from my imagine. I don't mind. That way the Crossroads is my place. I goes there and eat a frozen cup and every once or twice in a while, I let the Lady make me a po'boy. And she let me go in the back with the candles and such. I always feel that precious hand on my face. And the flames always dance a bit of a hello.

Mammaloose would have none of this coming my way if she knew about it. Even though I be nearly eighteen and in the last year of my high schooling, she tries to tell me every little thing to do. Or not to do. She be seeing me like she saw me at five years old.

After we finished the beans and rice, Mammaloose and Uncle Gilbert went to look at da TeeVee and I washed the dishes.

"Nuthin' 'bout no storm," Mammaloose called out.

"She bin right before," I heard Uncle Gilbert murmur.

When the kitchen was tidy the way Mammaloose likes, I left the house. I walked outside in the place where we live. Some would calls the day hot and humid. I say it's a different kind of rain. The air just can't let go of the water long enough for it to fall. That's what sweat is too, in a ways. Just rain popping out all over you.

I walked the place where I lives — I calls it my Garden of Neighbors — down toward JayEl's Daddy's Corner of Happiness Store. Some people talks about what ward they lives in. I don't do that. I heard Mammaloose once say that calling where you lives a ward make you sound like you living in some kind of institution. I can only be agreeing with her. I says I is a citizen of the Earth and right now I be living in a place somewheres between the old oak next to the yellow two-story and the gum tree out front of the pale green double shotgun. I lives in the place where the wisteria dips over the fence to hold hands with the magnolia that dips down to say hello to the Place Where My Vegetables Grow.

That's where I lives.

At Café Brouhaha, where I work, the owner's daughter, Louisa, asks me if I'm not afraid living where I lives. She thinks we killing each other all the time. I always tell her — 'cause she asks me a lot — I tell her, "Naw, that nonsense happens a few blocks down. We awright." She never seen violence where she live. It pretty all the time, I guess. I imagine my Garden of Neighbors likes that. I sees it all for what it truly is, I think. Like Mammaloose. I don't see her as bad. I'm not saying everything she does is good. Just like I'm not saying bad things ain't happening where I lives. I is saying other things going on too.

As I walked this place where I lives, I waved to Miss Sweet Desserts and Her Man Lionel. Miss Sweet Desserts used to calls me into her house every time I went by when I was small. She had cookies or pecan pie or beignets to hand out. She is the one taught me how to make beignets. She baked in the mornings 'cause she could not get to sleep after working all night. She was on one of those crews that cleans big old office buildings. All nights. Most every night. Now she happier, working days at Big Charity.

She says she don't mind sick people as long as she can sleep.

"You bring me by a beignet one of these days, sugar," Miss Sweet Desserts said.

"How ya doin'?" Her Man Lionel asked.

"I do fine," I said. "I come by tomorrow with some beignets."

I came upon Mr. Grant on his way home from looking for work. He walking. His car been down longer than the summer been hot, it seemed, and he run out of money now that the end of the month near.

"How you doing today, Mr. Grant?" I asks.

"I be fine," he said. "Worse than some, better than most. Can't complain."

"Any prospects today?"

He looking for a job longer than his car be resting. He hurt himself when he worked on one of the fishing boats.

"Prospects everywhere, *cher*," he said. "I just gotta find me one. You know what they says 'bout old Louisiana fishermen. We don't die. We just smell that way."

I laughs. It is not the first time I hears this joke from him.

"I got some okra in the Place Where My Vegetables Grow," I said. "You go on and get you some."

"I just might do that," he said. "Make me some jambalaya maybe. Invite over my lady friend."

I smiles. Mr. Grant always talking 'bout his lady friend. I never seen no one looks like a lady friend. I sometimes have the wonders if she real. But I imagine she a charmer, and that Mr. Grant has the happiest of times with her.

"You have yourself a night," I told him.

I waved to Mr. Grant and the Oak Tree and the Lincoln's Little Black Dog, who was nice enough to stay on his own steps and just wag his tail as I passed by. He couldn't see much these days, so his temper sometimes got the betters of him. He usually knew me by my smells, I suppose, but not always JayEl, so he nipped at his heels more than once. JayEl didn't like that much.

When I reached JayEl's Daddy's Corner of

Happiness Store, I saw JayEl leaning against the RTA sign out front, sucking on a frozen cup.

He held up his little finger, I linked my little finger with his, then we each pulled away.

He offered a frozen cup to me, but I shook my head.

"You afraid you catch something from me?" he asked.

I laughed. "I may be afraid of many things, but that ain't one of them."

We walked away from the corner and kept going until we come to the almost empty lot near the John the Baptist Church. Bottles and plastic bags and tall grass in the lot. We followed the path to the bench near the church. JayEl kicked litter out of our way.

"I always forget a bag so I can pick this stuff up," I says as we sat on the bench.

"You're not picking that stuff up," he said. "Could be needles and all kinds of things in there."

We been friends, JayEl and I, since we was way small, so he could say something like that to me

15

without sounding like he was bossing me. Other people sometimes talks to me likes I still small. Something about me or my words or my ways in the world they don't have an understanding for, I guess.

"You be my daddy now, JayEl?" I asked. "He protected me from all ways and means of bad things too once upon a times."

"Yeah, I be your daddy. And the sky is green."

"It probably is green somewheres," I said. "If you live under the water in the swamp and looks up, you'd probably think the sky is green."

"You might be right," he said. "Though I imagine it wouldn't be a good thing, otherwise, having a green sky. Not in normal life."

We watched the Mayeux brothers riding—and falling off—their boards. Hopping up and down. A breeze blew through so we couldn't hear their wheels hitting the pavement.

"You finish the history assignment?" JayEl asked.

"Sure. You?"

JayEl shrugged. He had troubles with motivation, especially motivating about stuff he didn't see as helping him.

"You know I don't like history," he said.

"History is just stories about what has already happened," I said. "You been here all your life; you know the stories. You the one who told me about the I-Ten columns. How the Old Oaks had made their homes in those spots where the columns are now. Those Old Oaks sheltered slaves and free black people for as long as anyone knows. Then the people built the I-Ten. They pulled up the trees and left them for dead. Dug up the neutral ground. Split the neighborhood. They put the cement columns where the trees had been. And one day the Artists came and did what they suppose to do in times like these: answer the call of the land, the community, and make beauty out of destruction, out of their imagines, out of what had been and was now. That's what they did."

JayEl and I have been to the concrete trees many times. Touching the painted worlds. Buying watermelons and veggies from the man playing chess.

"That's history," I said, "and you've told me that story many times."

JayEl laughed. "I'm not sure that story is gonna help me with my history assignment."

"She wanted us to write about a historical event. That was a historical event."

I likes thinking about those painted columns even if I wish the trees were there instead. I like the paintings all over our city. I especially like the big beautiful blue whales on the Whaling Wall on a hotel uptown. JayEl took me there the first time. I never seen any things so big and blue and watery as those whales. It seemed like those whales might swim right off the back side of the hotel.

"I bet if it ever floods here," I told JayEl then, "they be gone."

"I sure would be," he said.

JayEl always knows where the interesting is. And we friends for always. Was a few years where he was crazy over girls and he was getting into one trouble after another. Fighting. Growling territorial. His momma, Miss Celia Williams, work at the school.

She turn him around. Got him accepted to college for next year. Same as me, though he didn't get any gift of money like I did. Not many others we know have the same. Our school ain't the pretty place. Too much tough. Too much falling into parts. Not to my liking. But I figures out how to survive, how to put on my normal life, as JayEl calls it, when I'm there.

I was never crazy for boys—or girls—the way JayEl was crazy for girls. I be loving the ground and the sky and the trees and Samuel Beckett Sparrow and Miss Sweet Desserts and the Lady with the Galaxy in Her Eye and Mr. Lagniappe and Maya Angelou Hummingbird and JayEl—and Opal and Pearl, even though Mammaloose says they ain't real, they is part of my imaginings, too. I loves, but I never feels that crazy longing I seen in JayEl's eyes. It gone now. He got his reason back. I hope he still loves but not like before. Not like it was a cold he caught that made him all mean and sad and away from me.

I like JayEl 'cause he sees things. He says he likes me 'cause I paint pictures with my words. He says I talk like no other person he ever heard.

JayEl's momma was the one who said I was a citizen of the Earth; that's why I talk like people from all over. I likes when she put those words on me. I likes it fine. So I *be* a citizen of the Earth.

I almost told JayEl's momma about my sister Opal giving me the diary of Opal Whiteley. Least ways, that's what I believe happened. I found the book in a tin box in my locker, under some old clothes. I believes it come from the bayou with me. Opal Whiteley was a real life girl who lived up in the woods in the west corner of the U.S. of A. She talked to the trees and the animals likes I do. And she talked in the most beautiful ways. I have glad tidings each time I reads her. People thought she had the crazies, too. I have the thought that she a kindred spirit to me. She dead now. They put her in a place that had wards, and she died there.

JayEl says I paints pictures with my words like Opal Whiteley. He says I should write my imaginings. I have tried. Never turns out like my imaginings. It never has the beauty on the pages like it does in my head. So I figure other ways to make beauty.

At Tulane, I'm going to study bayous — swamps — and help them come back. They're like sponges, you know, swamps. They soak up water and keep the land from drowning. They soak up bad things so the land and us don't get sick. Right now, our city is sinking 'cause it's all wrong. Land needs to build up. That's what the Misi Sipi does. She brings all this sand and dirt out of her mouth and it build up the land. But the Misi Sipi don't work that ways anymore. She cut up. We cut off from her. No new land, so the city sinks.

When I tell Mammaloose I want to help the bayous, she says I got no sense. She thinks the whole city should sink. Sometimes I believes she wants everything to sink 'cause she feels like her whole life is nothing. It is a sad thing. JayEl doesn't understand why I'm not mad at Mamaloose all the times. I just isn't. I've felt afraid. Mostly I feel sad for her. But what can you do with another person's unhappiness? It ain't mine. She may want to give it to me, but I don't accept it. I don't want that gift. A gift can be a curse too. Can't it?

But that's beside what we was talking about.

"We gonna get a Big Spin," I told JayEl. "Ruby Butterfly told me and the trees told her."

JayEl looks over at me.

"It gonna be bad," I said. "It'll look like one of those spiral galaxies. And it'll be almost as big."

"They all look like galaxies," JayEl said. "Can't help but think how beautiful they are."

"Can't help," I agreed.

"Should I tell my mom?" he asked.

"You tell anyone you can," I said.

"You ever think maybe it's time we left here?"

JayEl was unsure of his place in this here galaxy. Or at least here here.

"You always wantin' to go someplace else," I said.

"Better than staying still," he said.

"Sometimes it's nice being still," I said. "You can hear the Flying People, feel the ground at your feet, the breath of the Rooted People on your skin."

"Yeah, I give you that. I also hear that couple in the corner house there screaming at one 'nother. I can smell oil or gasoline or exhaust from some old chevy, oil rig, or trawler. And that breeze is way wheezy and wet."

"You a half-frozen-cup-full kind of guy, ain't ya?" I said.

"Is this Big Spin the one?" JayEl asked. "The one that will bury us in water?"

"I don't think the Rooted People can see into the future," I said.

JayEl looked at me.

"They just know what's coming a little bit before everyone else," I said. "That's all."

JayEl laughed. "Guess psychic trees would be kind of strange. Wouldn't surprise me though."

"Though when I think about this hurricane coming," I said, "I think about the word *apocalypse*. It means 'to lift the veil.' Did you know that? Sometimes I feel like I got a veil over me, or like there is a veil over this whole city. I think the Big Spin might rip off that veil. And it ain't gonna be pretty, JayEl. At least not most of it."

"You think things will change?" JayEl asked. He shrugged. "Not much has changed here since slave times. Poor people are still poor people taking care of rich people."

"Those words have the truth all over them, Jay-El," I said. "Can't be arguing with you about that."

Just then, a hummingbird flies right up to our faces. She inches from us. We both so startled we stayed still. Seem like time stopped. Her rufous wings had the looksee of moving in slow motion. Her beak look like a needle. She look just like Maya Angelou Hummingbird, except Maya Angelou Hummingbird has a tiny white spot on her throat.

Then time started again, and the hummingbird flew away.

"What was that all about?" JayEl asked. "Another message from the trees? My momma says you're the only one she knows who gets hummingbirds in the summer. Now they're following you. What's that all about?"

"Maybe she was following you," I said. "You are pretty. They likes pretty."

JayEl grinned. "You think I'm pretty? I'm doin' all right then."

I laughed. "Wanna come watch while I clean out the hummingbird feeder? I think maybe it's time."

"Wouldn't miss watching you clean," he said. "I never seen one of them so close. They're so tiny." We gots up and started walking again.

"You sit on my steps out back and you see hummingbirds all the time."

"Never that close," he said.

"That's what comes from sitting still," I said.

"Uh-huh. I think maybe it has to do with your Big Spin. They want you to know it's coming."

"It ain't my Big Spin," I said. "I'm just the messenger."

CHAPTER 2

Twos Day

I DREAMED about whirlwinds again. Have you ever had that dream? It's not so bad. It washes everything away. Sometimes my family is in the whirlwind dreams too. Not Mammaloose or Uncle Gilbert but my true family. My momma, daddy, Opal, and Pearl. They beautiful, all. I'm trying to get to them in the dream. But I can't. Daddy is usually holding that little white Alley gator. His good luck. Then the whirlwind takes me away. Or takes them away. Last night it took us all.

I woke up with rain all over my body. I didn't see anyone when I gets up, didn't hear nothing. I went out to the Place Where My Vegetables Grow and sat on the ground. I asked if I could have a pepper, and then I plucked one off its stem and I ate it down. Samuel Beckett Sparrow came near and made some sounds. I looks over at him. He seemed his usual.

And the sky was so blue. All seemed like normal life. Maybe I was wrong about what Ruby Butterfly had to say to me.

"You have a good day, *mon amis*," I told Samuel Beckett Sparrow, the wisteria, the magnolia bush, and all my plants. "May everyone have the glad feels today."

Then I walked to the bus stop by the Corner of Happiness Store. It wasn't long in coming, that bus. I looked at all the people when I gots on. Some were longgoners. You know, those not quite all here here. Others smiled at me and asked how I was doing. I answered the same. Then I fall into another dream. Can't remember what it was. I wakes up at my stop, though, as was my usual. I thanked Mr. Driver and got off.

The bus rolls away. I wait until the fumes gone, then I breathe deeply and looks around. I likes coming up to the Vieux Carre. Always good smells: flowers, beer, and cinnamon all rolled together. Always be music. Even this early in the morning. I like the colors and the imaginings that life can be beautiful, even if it ain't always like that. But the poor and the rich get to walk in the beauty here. Dilapidated beauty is a good word to put on some of it. That's another one of those words I like. I like the sound. *Dilapidated:* it means "to fall into a state of disrepair" now. Long ago, it meants to scatter apart as if throwing stones. Some mornings I feel dilapidated. That could mean I feel like I am ruined or that I want to throw stones. Or I is scattered. Maybe all of it.

I like going to my job at Café Brouhaha. I come before school. Before most people awake. I walked down the block toward the café. A horse clip-clops down the road, no passengers, just the driver. That Beauty and her driver Mr. Beast. I wave. Beauty snorts, Mr. Beast nods. Too early for much speech. I go in the back way to the kitchen of Café Brouhaha.

No one there but Mr. Burden and Mr. Lagniappe —I forgot to say he works there too, got me the job. I calls Mr. Burden that 'cause everything seems likes it is such a burden to him. His daughter Louisa. His wife Minerva. (I loves her name. Seem like she should be a mermaid, don't it? She pretty. She pink and red. I swear one Mardi Gras she gonna turn into a fish or a mermaid or sumthin. I told her that one year, so she got herself a mermaid costume. We all had glad feels watching her that year.)

Mr. Burden has not many burdens, but he can go on and on about them. The government always doin' something to him. Some employee—he says it like, "Emm-ploy-eeeeee"—always stealing from him. Da ends of the worlds is always just around the corner. I tells him he should be full of cares going around any corners, the way he sees the world. He hardly understands a word I say. So I talk normal life with him when he is feeling most of his burdens. I can see he has a gratitude for that. I tells him he should learn to talk like me. Say whatever he wants whenever. Might lift a burden or more. I likes watching him with the customers. I'm usually in the back, but some mornings they need a little help out front—and some of the people knows me from being here so long. And they knows my beignets. Mr. Burden has the smile on all the time for his customers, even when he can't understand them. He been in Louisiana his whole life, like me, but sometimes the tourists talk too fast for him to be understanding. He just smiles, but I can see in his eyes he is scared because he is not knowing what is coming out of their mouths. He has me talk with them sometimes 'cause I kin understand words no matter who is putting them on and talking them out. English. French. Spanish. Some German. I'm not so good with the other languages. But dialects I get. Always been that way.

Mr. Lagniappe asks me how I'm doing and makes me café au lait. We sit at the long wooden table together and drink the coffee. I likes the chicory taste, but I don't much care for the coffee or the milk. I don't tell him this, though, 'cause it has become our routine, and if I gots up and started working, he'd do the same. Mr. Burden sat with us this morning, dunking yesterday's beignet in his coffee.

"I think Derek been takin' da butter and selling it on da streets," Mr. Burden said. "Down by da river."

"Who's been telling you that?" Mr. Lagniappe asked. "Derek never do such a thing. He an honest man."

I looked at Mr. Lagniappe. He shrugged. We both have a knowing that Derek ate way over his meal allowance. He says the allowance ain't fair. He a big man, big appetite. "You don't eat much," he tells me. "So I eat your share. And Big Bob. He don't eat nothing." That was all true, but he probably ate more than four people's share. He wouldn't be taking butter and selling it, though. That'd be too much trouble.

"Not Derek? Then who? We 'bout outta butter."

"Have you checked the invoice?" Mr. Lagniappe asked. "Maybe we didn't order enough butter or they didn't send enough."

Mr. Burden nodded. "Too much butter no good for ya. I hope I'm not killin' my customers." He slapped the table and got up and left the kitchen. Mr. Lagniappe and I laughs.

"What you want to do this morning?" Mr. Lagniappe asked.

"I figure the beignets and Linzer cookies," I said, "'less you need something else."

"That'll keep you busy before you catch the bus," he said. "Don't want you missing school."

"I got independent study after," I said. "By the park."

"What you studying there?" Mr. Lagniappe asked.

"The place," I said. "I'm studying ecology." That's another of those word I likes. Eeee-cology. It means "the study of the house of nature." *The house of nature.* Where is that? Isn't the house of nature everywhere?

"That sounds fine," Mr. Lagniappe said. "I'd like to have that independent study myself. If you done with that coffee, I'll finish it for ya."

I smiled and gives Mr. Lagniappe my coffee cup. Another one of our routines. That ways he can pretend he only having one cup instead of two.

"You ever hear of ecopsychology?" he asked. "Psychology is an interest of mine. My youngest daughter is studying it. She told me that ecopsychology combines your ecology with psychology. Says we as human beings can be inspired and healed by nature. Isn't that something? Seems like we already knew that, but people forget. Why do you suppose that is?"

"I don't know," I said. I was still back thinking about that word *ecopsychology*. I liked that. I likes the idea just fine. Healing by nature.

"If nature can heal us," I asked, "and I believe it can, what happens when nature is sick?"

"We have to feed the earth," Mr. Lagniappe said. "We have to take care of it. We're not separate from Nature, you know. We are Nature. Maybe you'll learn about all this in your independence study."

"Maybe I will," I said. "How's the wedding coming?"

Mr. Lagniappe's older daughter was getting married in November. He calls the older daughter Honey and the younger one Sugar. He says now that they is older they're not as fond of the names as they once were when they was younger.

"Everything is comin' along," he said. "Have I shown you a picture lately?" And he pulls out his wallet, opens it, and shows me a picture of all three of them together. I seen it before, but I didn't mind seeing it again. Every time Mr. Lagniappe takes out a new photograph of his daughters, I wonder if my momma and daddy ever did that. Did they have a favorite image of me they showed all around?

"Beautiful," I said. "You tell me when it is and I'll bake up something special."

"Maybe you'll come to the wedding," he said. "They're coming down here for it, and you'll get to meet them."

His daughters were away at college, one in Michigan, one in Texas.

"That'd be fine," I said.

He stared at the photograph for a moment, and then he put it away.

"You miss them?" I asked.

"I miss my daughters," he said. "I do. But we better get to work. I've got a wedding to pay for."

I made the Linzer cookies first. They easy. I combine the trinity of baking: sugar, fat, and flour, along with a few other ingredients. I rolled out the dough and cut it into heart shapes. Fake heart shapes. No real heart is shaped like a Valentine heart. At least not that I knows about. I put them on a cookie sheet.

Then I made a little well into each heart and dropped in some raspberry or strawberry preserves. Slid them into the big old oven. Rolled up the dough left over and started all over again.

Mr. Lagniappe baked bread. He sang a little. Turned on the news at the top and bottom of da hour. Or near enough. It was so low, I couldn't hear what they says. Then he'd turn it off. We both be liking the silence that wasn't real silence. We could hear things waking up from the open back door.

Eventually Miss Thelma would come back to ask how we doin'. But that wouldn't be until I made the beignets. Some people come into the café for their coffee and doughnut when they knew I was baking. They believe I use some kind of secret ingredients. I give them the list of what goes into them, but they think my beignets magic anyway. It's just that I sprinkle in cocoa powder with the powdered sugar. Nothin' fancy. Just cocoa.

Awright. I tells you, I do add a bit of nutmeg to that powdery sugar. And one more thing I use. I gets it at the Crossroads. It's chili pepper — a particular kind that comes from the country called Peru. I mix together powdered sugar, a pinch of nutmeg (or a bunch of pinches if I is making a big batch), cocoa, and a pinch of a pinch of the Peru chili pepper. I puts it all into the shaker that I use for my beignets.

Miss Thelma knows where the shaker is and so do the rest of the bakers and cooks, so they can use it anytime. But the customers can tell when I didn't bake the beignet. At least they say they can. I don't know why mine are different. Maybe it's because when I make the dough, I talk to it. I say, "I loves you. I loves you. I loves you." I do this 'cause once I heard a story about an old healer who would sit with a picture of someone, or a piece of cloth from the person who was in need of a healing, and she would say, "I love you, I love you, I love you. I'm sorry, I'm sorry, I'm sorry. I love you, I love you, I love you." Over and over. And the people would get well! So I do that when I bake. I do it other times too. Like at school if someone is putting words on me I don't like. (I say it quietly, mind you. I ain't a fool, no matter what people think.) Sometimes I do it with Mammaloose—

started that a couple years ago. Might been about the time she began to mellow. Although I would never use the word *mellow* to describe Mammaloose. But you get my ideas.

Miss Thelma and the breakfast cooks did come back to where Mr. Lagniappe and I was for a few minutes. We don't talks much. Did you notice cooks are often not happy people? At least not here-abouts. What's that mean? What a happy thing that is, to be passing your days making food for people. But they work too fast, it's way too hot, and Mr. Burden is himself a burden. So I lets the cooks be and they lets me be.

I made the beignets for an hour or more. Mr. Lagniappe always eats the first one of the day, Miss Thelma the second. Miss Thelma come and told me when Miss Jenine was out front, and I took her plate of three out to her special. Wasn't too busy on this morning. Light was bright outside. Already hot and sunny. Miss Jenine asked me to sits with her, but I don't. I never do. Mr. Burden 'bout have an attack if I did do.

"How's school, dawlin'?" she asked. She touched one of the beignets with her thumb and forefinger. She always asks me how school. "How ya mawmaw 'n' 'em?" she asks after Mammaloose. I tell her the same thing every time. "Still going to Tulane?"

"Next fall," I said.

"Good," she said. "I be watchin'. You make these beignets special for me?"

"Just for you," I told her.

Same thing every time. A routine. She always wink at me too. Looks me straight in my eyes.

"Come by soon," she said.

"I will," I said.

She owned a shop not too far from the café called Mask Her Aid. She had four walls of masks. Last Mardi Gras I got a hummingbird mask from her. I brought it back to her afterward, but she told me to keep it. I told her that Mammaloose has an allergy to pretty things. If she found it in my locker, she'd kill that hummingbird mask dead. I couldn't keep it. "I keep it for you," Miss Jenine said, taking the mask from me then. "I'll put it right up here and you can see it anytime."

Just now, I thought maybe I should tell her about the Big Spin. Thought about telling Mr. Lagniappe too. But I didn't. I went back and finished my work, got a few beignets for Miss Sweet Desserts, then went to the park: home of the Old Oaks and the Flying Horses. Being in the park in the almost-wilds fills me with glad feels. I hoped the Big Spin wouldn't hurt this place.

Later, after school, I stops by the Corner of Happiness Store with JayEl. His daddy, Benjamin, sometimes makes us po'boy when no one else is around. Sometimes he gives away frozen cups to every child that comes near on the bad hot days. "Some of those kids can't afford to take a breath," he says, "so I can treat them if I have a mind to." Mr. Benjamin has a kind mind. Sometimes the world seems all full up of kindness. Other times . . . well, you know.

Then I walked to Miss Sweet Desserts's house and stepped up on her porch, where she sat fanning herself. Her house has a big ole porch on it. Doesn't quite fit the rest of the house. It made of rocks and concrete, solid and straight on. The house a bit crooked. Reminds me of a woman I seen at church a few years back, when we still go. Mrs. Rogeau. She so poor you could see through her dresses if you had a mind to—even if you didn't, if the light was just wrong. But she had the prettiest hats. Funny hats. Some of those kids—you knows the kind—they make fun of her. They just as poor. Don't know what they fussing after her about. Some of the hats looked as though they made of felt. Soft smooth. Most had a feather or more sticking out of them. One even had a wren on it. I swear. I look real close to make a certainty it was not real. She say to me, "Ruby Marie, you knows me better than that!" Mrs. Rogeau. She dead now. So I walks up onto the porch that reminds me of Mrs. Rogeau and handed Miss Sweet Desserts her bag of beignets.

"You want I go in and get you a plate?" I asked. "They from the morning. Not the freshest."

"They be fine," Miss Sweet Desserts said. "I eat

them right here. Thank ya, dawlin'. I hear they got themselves one of those almost-hurricanes by the Bahamas. They calls it Tropical Depression Twelve. Now ain't that a catchy name? You hear anything?"

I shrugged. Almost said, "Just what the little butterfly tells me." But I don't say a thing. Miss Sweet Desserts gets spooked easily.

"Probably won't touch us," she said. "We be fine."

CHAPTER 3

Thirst Day

FELT UNCOMMONLY HOT when I woke. Mammaloose was in my locker, pulling out clothes like she her own Big Spin.

"What you lookin' fer?" I pressed my hands against my eyes for a moment, trying to bring backs whatever dream I was having. It was better than Mammaloose wrecking my room.

"None of your business," Mammaloose said. "This is my house! Mine. You're lucky I let you live in it."

I gots out of my little bed that comforts me every night and I pulls on the slacks that I had left hanging on the Three-legged Chair JayEl Found in one of the empty lots a year or so back. Should be four legs, but we hadn't found the right artificial leg yet, so I left it just as is, green paint peeling off it. I gots to be full of care that it don't tip right over. I puts my clothes on it just so. I leaned over and took a shirt from the pile of clothes on the floor. I don't have that many clothes, so that they could make themselves into a pile was a surprise to me.

"I'm just saying I could help you," I said, "if I know what you need."

"My chartreuse scarf," she said. "The one Mamma Rose left me."

"I haven't seen that since she died," I said. Which was long times ago. Mammaloose weren't looking for no scarf.

"This is my house and you will do what I say," she said. She turned to me and put her hands on her hips. She gots steam coming out of her. Be it her rain turning to mist or something else, I didn't know.

"You stay away from that Jacob Williams."

"Mammaloose, he be my friendliest friend in the whole world," I said.

"Don't you talk that Ruby garbage talk with me," she said. "That boy was caught with his gangsters breaking in to the school. They say they were looking for drugs."

"If they were looking for drugs, they wouldn't go to the school at night," I said, putting on my most normal words—although if my words sound likes the people on da TeeVee, Mammaloose would get on her even madder face, thinking I be putting on airs. You ever wonders what that means? Putting on airs. Could I be putting on fires? Waters? Earth? Would those be good things to be putting on? Does it mean I be dressing in air that wasn't meant to be mine?

"Jacob doesn't do drugs," I said.

"If I ever catch you around someone who does drugs, you're out in the street, you understand me?"

"Mammaloose, you taught me better than that," I said. I wanted to say my momma and daddy taughts me best, 'cause Mammaloose taughts me how to be full of the fears. I am still taking off those fears.

"I don't want that Jacob boy anywhere near you," Mammaloose said.

She stomps out of my room. Just like a big ole child stompin'. I picked up my shirts one by one and hung them up again. What she looking for in my locker? Drugs? JayEl? I don't go after her to beg her to let me see JayEl likes I would have done when I was small. I ain't gonna stop seeing JayEl. That would be likes not seeing the sky. It is not in my imagining. I will find out the truth and then hand it to her. Get JayEl's momma to call her. Mammaloose like her. Mammaloose always be full of fears about drugs. She says they ruin families, neighborhoods. I agree with Mammaloose about this. She should knows I wouldn't be around drugs or anybody looking for or doing them. Not JayEl either.

I tidied up the Place Where I Dream. Then I went outside to the Place Where My Vegetables Grow. Samuel Beckett Sparrow flew down to the wisteria and looked at me.

"Joyful morning to you," I said. I did a looksee at the Feeder for the Flying People hanging near the Place Where My Vegetables Grow. It gots plenty of seeds. Then I leans down and asks the pepper plants if I can have a couple for Mammaloose. She loves munching on them. I takes two, says goodbye to Samuel Beckett Sparrow, and walks back to the house. Maya Angelou Hummingbird is at her Feeder of the Humming Flying People by the door. She be trying to chase away a smaller hummingbird with the glitters on it.

"Maya Angelou," I said, "you play nice and share."

She ignored me. I don't think that Maya Angelou Hummingbird has an understanding of human language, not likes Samuel Beckett Sparrow. He seems to want to listen to me talk all day long—not that I would do that. I wouldn't have a wanting to bore him. I mean, birds can fly. They can touch the sky. I needs to be interesting, you know, so he don't roll his eyes when talking with his friends, telling them how that human Ruby can talk the whole days long about no thing at all. So I tells him jokes. Or about Mr. Lagniappe. Or the Lady with the Galaxy in Her Eye. Miss Sweet Desserts. Or JayEl.

Maya Angelou Hummingbird and the glitter hummingbird flew away as I went into the house. I walks into Mammaloose's kitchen.

"I got these for you," I said, holding out the red peppers from my garden. Treasures.

"You trying to give me heartburn?" Mammaloose asked. She stood at the stove frying eggs. "Put those grits on a plate for your Uncle Gilbert."

Uncle Gilbert looked up at me from his paper. He usually not up this early.

"How ya doin', Ruby?" Uncle Gilbert said. "I take the peppers if she don't want 'em."

I got a plate for Mammaloose and one for Uncle Gilbert. Then I takes the pot to the table and spooned out the grits (with cheese and onions). I gave over the peppers to Uncle Gilbert. They likes being eaten by him anyway, I decide. I feel the cloth around my neck—like things is getting hot or uncomfortable. I got the angry feels for Mammaloose. JayEl asks me one time if I knows why Mammaloose did not have the liking of me. I said I never knew. I guess I just born that way. He says, "You not born no way but good; something wrong with Mammaloose she don't likes you."

He be right. He be right.

"You ain't eatin' with us?" Uncle Gilbert asked.

"I'm going to work," I said.

"You remember what I says about that Jacob boy," Mammaloose said, her back to me.

"I didn't hear no thing that made a lick of sense to me," I said. "So I am surely not gonna remember it."

Mammaloose's back stiffened. If I were younger, I knew she would have taken her hand across my face. Uncle Gilbert got real quiet-like. Reminded me of a rabbit I seen at the Home of the Big Oaks and the Flying Horses. Think if he be all silent and still no one will see his shivers.

Then Uncle Gilbert said, "Seems like they think that storm gonna become a hurricane."

Mammaloose began stirring the eggs again. "You come by the hotel after school and help out, Ruby."

Once a week I goes to Mammaloose's hotel, the one where she works, and helps her. She's in charge of keeping the house. More and more she don't like the paperwork, so I helps out. She tells everyone it a school thing. She helping me out, she says. Giving me experience.

"I can't come today," I told her.

Then I took one of the peppers off of Uncle Gilbert's plate and left the house before I says something that would cause Mammaloose to want to hit me or put me out of the house. Mammaloose always threatening to throw me out. Ever since I was small. That put the fear on me in the way back. She kept talking about me living on the streets. I had the imagining that cars would run over me while I sleep.

One morning real early, I went and sat outside on the street to see if I could live there. I wanted to be prepared. Yes, sir. I sat on the street for hours. No body seemed to notice. The cars, well, they went around me, either with a purpose or because they had no noticing of me. It was a hot day. I brought no water or food because Mammaloose says she would send me out with none. She says I would only have the clothes on my back. So that's the way I sat in the street. Sometime during the day, I starts seeing things as they are in the true world. I see the cars as people flying down the street. I see the trees moving and bending and pulsing and rooted. I see and hears the birds talking to each other and with me. I feel the wind try to cool my forehead. I feel the earth trying to come up through the road and put a comfort on me. I hear the whispers of my sisters telling me that one day they come back for me, one day they find me. I hear the sun way up there telling me to gets away and find me some shade. Shadow a good thing, child, the sun says. Gets away, dawlin', gets away. And then I hear the whispers of people. "She passed out, poor thang." "Get her inside." "What she up to out here like this?" "Mammaloose gonna whip her fer sure."

I didn't get a whipping that time. Mammaloose took good cares of me for the few days I was in bed. After that, I sees the world like it truly is. At least that is what I have a thinking I do. And the Lady with the Galaxy in Her Eye has an agreement with me on this. She say, "You don't judge people, *cher*. You see right to their true spirit. You see how it is. Good or bad." Not everyone sees things that way. Probably why I don't have the angry feels very often. Most people don't mean no harm. I don't mean by this that I stands by and let someone hurt someone else just because I see the hurting person ain't that bad. The person putting on the hurt needs to be stopped. I just ain't full of hate for him while I be telling him to stop hurting.

With Mammaloose it be harder to tell her to stop. It harder because she supposed to love me. She don't. She supposed to like me. She don't. I never had no body 'cept her since my daddy and momma died. I don't have a hankering to sleep on the streets. But I don't believe I wants to tolerate her meanness no more.

I bit into the pepper as I walked toward the bus stop. It were bitter. Not a good bitter like lettuce or dandelion. I ate it anyway. I have a hoping that the bitters got honeyed by my natural sweet nature. That idea gives me a smile I take all the way to the bus stop.

Mr. Lagniappe could see I did not have on my glad feels, and he made me calas for breakfast. He can cook and bake.

"You make someone a fine husband," I tells him. "The Lady know you cook?"

Mr. Lagniappe smiled as he sipped his café au lait.

"Why you mention the Lady?"

"Just saying. These good. Mmm-mmm."

"What happened to you this morning got you all different?" Mr. Lagniappe asked.

"Mammaloose accused JayEl of breaking in to the school and doing drugs," I said. "She don't know nothing about such things."

"You know he didn't do it?"

"Course I knows," I said.

"Didn't he get into trouble way back?"

"Yes, he did," I said. "But like you says, it was in the way-back time. He don't do such things."

"You talk to him?"

"Just found out," I said. "But I don't need to."

"I hear ya," he said. He nodded. "You a good judge of character, Ruby. I always think so."

"Can I help with the bread today?" I asked.

"Sure, you wanna punch some dough?"

"Seem like the thing to do."

I did not see hairs or hide or limbs or anything else belonging to JayEl at school. I hears the others talking about some bodies breaking into the school. I was surprised to hear they actually locks the school. It been a good building once, it had the prospects, but now it is raggedy as a doll been in the mouth of a big ole alley gator, I'm telling you. I look for Miss Williams, JayEl's momma, but she gone too.

I took a bus to the Home of the Big Oaks and the Flying Horses after my classes. I went straight on to the oaks and cypress trees growing up along what is left of the Bayou Metairie. I go quiet. I ask one of those big old live oaks if I might have lunch sitting by it. I hear no protests, so I sits down beside it, in its shade, thanking it, and I watch the ducks and swans floating by. Sometimes I gets one of those little boats and goes out into these lagoons and floats in the water alongside the birds. I have the imagines that I am in a boat with my sisters and daddy and momma. I wouldn't swim in that water. I don't know how to swim. At least I don't think I do. Do people who lives in the bayous know how to swim? Or do they know better than to get into the water? I have thought about this before. I figures if I get thrown into the water, I'll know what to do. Or else I won't. No sense fussing about it now.

Mammaloose never let me swim in no public pools. Said the one at the Audubon park wasn't for us. She had this little plastic pool that Uncle Gilbert would blow up—he'd get so out of breath trying to blow that thing up for me. I would just laugh. He never got it tight, but it held the water anyway and I gots cooled down on the hot summer days. But I didn't learn to swim.

On this day, I sits by the swamplike place under this grand old oak, eating my cold calas and beignets —and an apple—wondering where JayEl has gotten himself. I should go to his house and knock on his door, but I wouldn't want him to think I had the doubts on me about him.

I gots out my notebook and I used my colored pencil to take a picture of all that I seen. It was a slow process and it didn't look like it would if I had had a camera, but I gets to know it better doing it this way. Then I wrote me some notes. About the way the swan cleaned herself. About the way the Big Oak never seemed to move but how I could feel the old tree pulsing way deep down, same with the cypress. The trees all said the same thing: Hang on, hang on, hang on for your dear dear dearest life. And the moss hanging from the cypress like some kind of filigreed nature shawl shivered even though not even a whisper of a whisper of a breeze was running about, like the exclamation at the end of a sentence filled with greatness of import. Maybe the Big Spin that Ruby Butterfly told me about didn't have anything to do with the hurricane that was or was not heading toward that state called Florida. Maybe the Big Spin was more personal, like toward me. Maybe something was gonna happen to JayEl.

I did not like the direction my thinking was going. It was times like this when I have the thoughts that I should put on the normal life all the time.

Maybe I don't want to hear what the butterflies or Rooted People or Flying People be saying. 'Specially if it be always bad stuff.

I closed my eyes and leaned back against the Big Oak. I felt its liveliness up against my back and I was all smiles again. And I breathed in deeply all those airs; whether they be mine to put on or not, I breathed them in. I looks around at this place beautiful and I whispers, "Thank you, thank you, thank you."

CHAPTER 4

Fried Day

THIS HERE was a peculiar day. I never did hears from JayEl. I stopped by his daddy's corner store, but the daddy and JayEl gone and no body knew no thing. At work, Mr. Lagniappe and Miss Thelma talked about the Big Spin.

"Only a category one and it ripped parts of Florida pretty hard," Miss Thelma said. "Good thing it ain't comin' this way. And even if it does, I am about ready for a hurricane party."

"*Laissez les bons temps rouler,*" Mr. Lagniappe said.

"Your mouth to God's ear," Miss Thelma said.

At school, no JayEl. I calls his house again. No answer.

Everyone says he in jail.

I asked his other friends. They says they don't know where he gone to.

At lunch I asks my teacher if I could please go do my independent study. I try not to let her sees the tears in my eyes, though I was ready to tell her it was just rain — or what she would call sweat. My eyes were just sweating. It was so hot in that school. She let me go. Told me to have a good weekend. Put her hand on my shoulder when she says the words.

I went by the store again, but no one was there I know, and they knows nothing about JayEl and his dad.

"I don't keep track of boss man," the boy at the counter said, and he laugh like he the most clever person on the planet. He not from around here. We take better cares of each other than that.

I took the bus up to the park. I have my imaginings that I would work. I read some about ecology, how it's all intertwined, how we all a part of each other, though they didn't say it quite that way, and I leaned against the Big Oak and watched the swans. My stomach had the bad feels. I remembered these bad feels from when I first came to Mammaloose's house—when my momma and daddy died. I don't mean I remember what happened. I just remember living with Mammaloose and having no glad tidings for a while. I remember no more smells of the bayou. No more white alley gator. No more army dillos. No more jewels: Opal and Pearl. I wish I remembered them in real life. Wish I could see them in my mind.

A few years ago I went looking to find out about my sisters Opal and Pearl. I went through Mammaloose's belongings every time she at work. I never found no thing about me or my family. That's when I starts having big doubts about my remembering. Maybe I did make them all up. Mammaloose never whipped me for going through her things, so I must have done a good job making it all tidy again. Or it might be she just never thought I would do such a thing like that. She sees me like a mouse for so many years.

Back then, I asked Miss Sweet Desserts what she knows about my family, but she gets all quiet every times and says she don't know nothing. My daddy and mommy were good people and they went away. Did I have sisters? Sisters? No, dawlin', she says, I don't remember any sisters.

A woman used to live in that camelback down the street now owned by Mr. and Mrs. Conners from Boston. Her name be Emmy Pea, and she said she knew my momma and daddy. "You daddy tall and lanky," she said, "real handsome. He could wrestle an alligator and win—using his charm. You momma beautiful too. She have some trouble but she try hard." "What about my sisters?" "I don't know about you sisters, dawlin'." She never told me any more even though I took care of her lawn for a summer and sometimes sat with her on her steps while she drank Coke with something extra in it, smoked her cigarettes, and told me about her boyfriend. Mammaloose didn't like me knowing her. She afraid she gonna give me drugs or alcohol, I guess. I was ten years old. Who gonna do that? Course, Uncle Gilbert tried to give me beer more than once in my life. Just to be polite, he said, not 'cause he bad. Miss Emmy Pea did not stay around long. She couldn't pay her rent and she gone one day. I likes her. She had green eyes. I never seen no one with green eyes before. Never has to this day. Not like hers. Like they had a tiny light behinds them. Kind of like the Lady with the Galaxy in Her Eye, only she more here, the Lady, and Miss Emmy Pea couldn't sit still, and she hardly ever looked me in the eyes herself. I have the sad feels for her.

Just like now I have sad feels. I wonder about JayEl. I think about getting up and walking to the stone bridge I likes—it looks like a raised eyebrow made out of stone, or like a cattypillar arching up over the water. I likes standing on the hump above the water—I have the feels then that I is putting on airs and waters. I am about to gets up and do all that when I hears, "There you are. I been looking all over for you."

I looks up. JayEl stands over me. He holds out his little finger to me. I takes it with my own, then we pulls away.

JayEl tries to give me a frozen cup. I just looks at him.

"Well, take it," he said. "I figured I'd find you here, so I bought you one. You know I don't like raspberry."

I takes it from him, and he sat next to me and leaned up against that old live oak. He look good by that big old tree and not in jail.

"Where you been?" I asked.

"My aunt had a baby up in Baton Rouge," he said. "Mom made us all go. Be with family. Had some good celebratin' food. I called Thursday, told your mawmaw."

"She must have forgot to say," I said. "This good frozen cup. You get it on the corner?"

"You know I did," JayEl said. "And you know your mawmaw didn't forget nothing. She a mean old bat. You worried about me? I heard Tyrone and his boys got caught breaking in to the school. They said I was with them. Everyone in the school believes it, I hear. None of them knew we were gone, I guess. You believe it?"

He looks over at me, sidelong, biting on his snoball.

"Mammaloose believed it," I said. "I wondered why she didn't fuss about you when I came home Thursday. Before that she said I couldn't be around you no more."

"What'd you tell her when she said that?"

"I said it wasn't true. I knew none of it was true."

"But you still worried. I can see that. You know I can take care of myself."

"I worried because I didn't know where you were," I said. "You're my best friend and you disappeared for two days. You could have been in jail like the wrong man or something."

"Funny how when you get mad your words go all normal life," he said.

I looks at the swans on the water. I feels my heart in my chest.

Finally I said, "I can take other people making fun of me. I can take my grandmother being mean to me. I can take life just as it is. But you making fun of me ain't gonna be part of it."

"I wasn't making fun," JayEl said. "I think it's charmin' that you were worried."

I looks over at him. He is grinning, munching on his frozen cup.

"You being strange," I said. "Why'd Tyrone say you did it?"

He shrugged. "Tyrone thought I was playing with his girl."

"Playing with his girl? Playing music? Playing golf?" I asked.

JayEl laughed.

"And *his* girl. He be owning people now?"

"You know what I mean," he said.

"You be playing?"

"Naw."

"None of my business," I said. "You like his girl-friend, you go for it. I just don't want you to go all crazy again."

He shook his head. "Must be nice not feeling that way about nobody."

"What you mean?"

"You, you know. At least you never told me if you liked someone."

"I likes lot of people," I said. "I don't know what you talkin' about."

"Playing dumb? That ain't my Ruby. No sir. You know what I'm talking about."

"I can't help it if I never had a crush on some *one*," I said. "I've got a crush on the whole world."

JayEl nodded. "I know, I know. Must get lonely sometimes though."

"Lonely?" I shook my head. "I gots you, JayEl. How could I be lonely?"

"I'm not gonna be around forever," he said. "We're going to college next fall."

"We're going to the same school," I said.

He sighed.

"Yeah, I know," I said. "You'll go have your life and I'll go have mine. We be friends, though, even if we're not together."

"Ruby, Ruby."

"What?"

"No thing at all," he said.

"I'm glad you aren't in jail. I'm glad you didn't do it."

"I'm glad that baby was born," he said. "If I'd been here, everybody would have believed it, probably even my parents. Except you. I knew you'd know it wasn't me."

"I knew."

We looked at each other. I smiled. JayEl picked a leaf out of my hair. He had the looks like he wanted to say more, but he got up and reached for my hand. I gives it to him, and he pulled me up.

"Let's go ride the flying horses," he said. "I'll treat."

"It's always a treat to be with you," I said, "and the flying horses."

And we ran away from the tree and the water—I waves goodbye to them—just like we was kids again, laughing and playing with each other in the park. Like old times all over again.

We stopped by the corner store after. Mr. Williams sat on his stool, looking at the teevee.

"I was just about to make myself a po'boy," he said to us. "Don't tell your momma. You want one?"

JayEl and I says we wouldn't mind a po'boy. I used the telephone to call Mammaloose and let her know I wasn't coming home for dinner, just to be polite, and maybe to let her know I was at the corner store with JayEl and his daddy. They be back from Baton Rouge where they been for the last two days, I said. I be home when I gets home. Though I was nice about how I said it. The store was empty of people 'cept us, so we sat at the counter eating and looking at the teevee.

"That storm is a hurricane again," Mr. Williams said. "They think it's coming toward Louisiana. The governor's declared a state of emergency."

JayEl looked at me. I shook my head. I didn't want him telling his daddy what Ruby Butterfly had told me.

"Ruby thinks this is gonna be a big one," JayEl said.

Mr. Williams nodded. "I think you might be right, Ruby girl. Your momma called, JayEl, and wants us to come to Baton Rouge. Maybe I'll put you on a bus tomorrow."

"Naw," JayEl said. "We been through this before. I'll stay here and help you out."

"We'll see how it goes," he said. "Your momma is happy to spend more time with her sister. Store gets pretty busy just before a storm though."

"Good," JayEl said. "I can make some extra money!"

"Have they been saying we should all leave?" I asked.

"Not that I heard," Mr. Williams said. "It won't come here. Pass us right by, I figure. We need to get everything boarded up just in case."

"Tonight?" JayEl asked.

"We'll wait and see which way the wind is blowing tomorrow," Mr. Williams said. "Could still turn."

"I'll bring you some beignets from Café Brouhaha tomorrow," I said. "I'll help some if you need it."

"We'll look out for each other," Mr. Williams said. "It'll be fine."

"That was a good po'boy, Mr. Williams," I said. "Thank you. I best be gettin' home. I'll see you tomorrow."

"Yeah, if the Big Spin doesn't spin us all away," JayEl said.

He winks at me. I have glad feels that nothing bad happened to JayEl. I went outside and walked toward Mammaloose's house. I felt the shivers all over. I realized the Big Spin was coming our way and nothing was going to be normal life again.

CHAPTER 5

Sad Turn Day

I AWAKES with *the* most full of wonders feels. You knows what I mean? Likes the whole of the universe is waiting on me, arms open. And can you have an imagine how many arms the Universe would be having? So I gots out of bed and danced around my tiny Place Where I Dream in Mammaloose's house, my bare feet likin' the feel of the wood beneath it, moving just a bit from my weight, bending a little, letting me knows it likes it, too, the wood, I mean, the house, every bit of the world likes my dance, and as I whirl, I put the picture in myself of the Big Spin getting smaller and smaller, till it just a pretty dot of spin, like a spider web.

Then I dress myself and go into the blue sky day and out to the Place Where My Vegetables Grow. I waits for Samuel Beckett Sparrow, but he doesn't come. No birds at the Flying People Feeder. I looks over at Maya Angelou's feeder. No bodies there either. I walked to the bus stop by the Corner of Happiness Store. JayEl and his dad were putting boards up on the windows of the store. They about the only ones. I didn't see no body else doing much of no thing in my Garden of Neighbors.

"How ya doin'?" JayEl asked as he jumped down from the ladder.

"I never seen you up this early in your life," I said.

Mr. Williams laughed as he hit the nails on their heads. "Yeah, you right 'bout that," he said.

"Did you hear it's headed this way?" JayEl said. "And it's big."

"Are you gonna go to Baton Rouge and be with your momma?" I asked.

"She wants us to go," he said. "Dad wants to stay for a while."

"I'll see you after work then," I said. "If you're still here."

"Stop by," JayEl said.

I nodded.

The bus pulled up and I got on. I watched JayEl and his father until they were out of sight.

In the Vieux Carre, the sound of hammering and drilling filled the air like the din of all kinds of birds in the trees waiting to migrate. I stood still and listened for a minute before going into the back of the restaurant.

Everything different as soon as I steps inside. Miss Thelma, Mr. Burden, the morning cooks, and Mr. Lagniappe were all there working.

"We opened early," Mr. Burden said to me, "and we're boarding up and closing after breakfast. I want everyone to have enough time to get out of town."

"You look surprised, dawlin'," Miss Thelma said. "You know that hurricane is heading here and it's a category three and expected to get bigger. It is time to get out of Dodge."

"I didn't know you ever closed," I said.

"Louisa and Minerva are packing up our things at home, and we're leaving just as soon as we can," Mr. Burden said. "You should too."

I went to stand at Mr. Lagniappe's side. I had the bad feels and thought he would be steadier than Mr. Burden.

"What you want me to do?" I asked him.

"Make the beignets," he said. "Make some extra to take with. I'll give you some bread too."

"You leaving the city?" I asked.

"We'll see what happens," he said. "We been through this before."

"I think it's going to be big and it's going to be bad," I said. "I think we should all leave."

I didn't knows I was gonna say that until the words came out of my mouth. Mr. Lagniappe looks at me.

"You know something?" he asked.

"Just what the butterfly and the trees told me," I said.

He nodded.

"Well, then, we best get to work."

We baked and fried and bagged. Miss Jenine came in for her beignets, but she wanted to take them with her. I went out front to say hello. The café was full of people; outside, people walked around in the sunshine.

"How you doin', Ruby dawlin'?" she said. "You ready for the storm?"

I didn't know how to answer that.

"How about you?" I asked.

She shrugged. "I'll move some things off the floor, then look for a party." She smiled. "I live above the store, and this here is higher ground. I'll be awright. You get yourself right now."

I handed her the bag of beignets. "I will," I said.

"Come by after and see the hummingbird," she said. "We'll all have stories to tell."

I watched her leave the restaurant and walk out into the street. She wobbled slightly, like her heel caught on something, then she keep going. She walk pretty, just like she looked.

We lifted bags and boxes up off the floor and anything else we could think of. Mr. Burden closed the restaurant and told us we could go; they would board up the windows. Mr. Lagniappe offered me a ride home. I took it with glad feels. I didn't want to miss JayEl before they left for Baton Rouge. I got into his old white pickup and he drove us to the Crossroads first.

Two people I did not know was making po'boys and sno-balls and taking money from the people in line who was stocking up before the Big Spin. I follows Mr. Lagniappe to the back, where the candles and the pictures were. He stopped before going in. He calls out, "You there?"

"I'm here," the Lady says. "Come on."

Mr. Lagniappe let me go in first. The warm air washed across my face as always. I walks past the altar and sees that the Lady and a young man I don't know are stacking sacks of rice, flour, beans up off the floor.

"Go on and bring in the water," she says to the young man. He leaves out the back. "How you two doin'?"

"Mr. Lagniappe taking me home," I said. "The café closed until after."

She nodded. "We're gonna do a ceremony tonight. You welcome to come, *cher*, you still in town. We do some dancing!"

"You need help with this here?" Mr. Lagniappe asked.

The Lady looked at him like she was trying to figure out something.

"Well, Mr. Lagniappe, you always good at finding stuff," she said. "If I think of anything I'll let you know."

"I can help board up the place," he said.

"I won't say no to that," she said. "You take Ruby home and come on back if you got the time." She came and put her arm across my shoulder. "You don't stay too long, *cher*. Sometimes the best thing is to leave."

Mr. Lagniappe dropped me off at the corner store. Lots of people were making groceries. I went inside to find JayEl but he was working. We looked at each other. I mouthed that I was going home. See ya later, gator, I whispered. After a while, crocodile, he mouthed. Just like when we was kids. We looked at each other for a second. Then someone caught JayEl's attention and I left. I stopped by Miss Sweet Desserts on the way home. She and Her Man Lionel were looking at the teevee.

"The mayor gonna speak soon," Miss Sweet Desserts said. "We been listening to the radio. This storm is big. You see it?"

I shook my head.

"There it is," Her Man Lionel said.

I looked at the teevee and saw this huge white galaxy-shaped thing filling up the screen. It was beautiful. And butterflies in my stomach started flapping their wings like I was a cage and they wanted out.

"You need anything?" I asked.

"Naw," Her Man Lionel said. "We got what we need for the next couple days."

"When's it going to get here?" I asked.

"Looks like Monday," Miss Sweet Desserts said. "You come over before or after and we cook us up a bunch of treats."

I handed her a small bag of beignets.

"I'll talk to you later," I said. "Your phone back working yet?"

"Uh-huh," Her Man Lionel said. "Mr. Grant comin' by later and we play some cards. Have ourselves our own little hurricane party."

"You got your medicine?" I asked.

"I asked him the same thing," she said.

"Everybody out making groceries, getting gas," he said. "I'll go after. I gots enough for now. You women always fussin'."

Miss Sweet Desserts raised an eyebrow. "Yeah, well, last time we had water up the steps. This one look a little bigger."

"I better go see if Mammaloose needs me," I said.

I stood on Mrs. Rogeau's Hat Porch for a minute and looks around at this place where I lives. Some people walking, some talking, on their boards, dancing. Sun shining. Sky blue. No birds. I looks out where the Big Spin was supposed to come, and I sees just blue skies. Maybe nothing gonna happen, I thinks. No storm coming. It so pretty today, like Miss Jenine's walk.

Maybe we'll all go on as before.

I run home. Uncle Gilbert is eating a sandwich while he look at the teevee.

"Where's Mammaloose?"

"They got her working," he said.

"Didn't they send all the tourists home yet?" I asked. "The café is closed."

"Naw. They don't want to scare them tourists away for good," he said.

"Have you seen how big the hurricane is?" I asked.

"Yep. They gonna have a bigger scare if them tourists all dead," he said. He chuckled. "I hear they gonna close down the gas stations. I better go fill up the car case we leave town."

"You ever left town before?" I asked.

"Betsy," he said. "I was just a little older than you is now. Good thing we left. Our house was flooded. My granddaddy stayed and he almost drowned. Had to chop his way out of the attic."

"Should we do something here to get ready?" I asked.

He shrugged. "You know as much as I do. Don't want to do anything to set off Mammaloose. Moving stuff and the likes."

"Should we board up the house?"

"Probably," he said. "Maybe I go around the block and see if I can scare up some wood."

He got up out of his chair slowly and tooks his empty plate into the kitchen.

"Your grandmama be home soon," he said. "She'll tell us what to do."

He got a beer from the refrigerator, then went back to look at the teevee.

"I'm going to the corner store," I said.

"Good idea," he said. "You make some groceries."

I still felt the bad feels, and I couldn't stay inside and do nothing. The line was still long at the store. Everyone was talking and joking. I hears them and I feels calm again, likes it would all be fine. I went inside the store. JayEl smiles when he sees me.

"I can help," I said.

I'd done it before. I knew how to make the sno-balls and the po'boys and change. I knew where most everything in the store was. I went behind the counter and stood between Mr. Williams and JayEl, and I helps. We works as a team, the three of us. Every body in the store and out was like friends, and I feels a little likes I is at a party. I had glad feels that I was feeding people and helping them find what they has a need for.

"Shhh!" someone said. "The mayor is speaking!"

Mr. Williams turned up the radio and we all listened.

"We strongly advise citizens to leave at this time," the mayor said.

JayEl and I looked at each other. Ruby Butterfly seemed to have more urgency on her than he did.

"We want everyone to not panic but to take this very seriously. Every projection still has it hitting New Orleans in some form or fashion."

"What that mean, 'form or fashion'?" someone say.

"Shhhh!" Someone else.

Soon it seemed everyone was talking. Then Mr. Williams held up his hand for quiet again. The governor was speaking. She told us to go door to door and tell people they need to gets out of town.

"They didn't say we *has* to leave," someone said. "So it don't mean nothing. Nothing can be that big."

"It's big," someone else said. "All those levees they didn't give no money to over the years like they says they would. They all gonna go."

"Or they could blow them up like they did during Betsy."

"Why they do that?"

"Drown all the poor people, that's why!"

"Who'd they get to wait on them then?"

Laughter.

The line moved on. The press conference ended. At least as far as I knew. I could tells that Mr. Williams was listening to the radio even as he was getting the people what they needed. He had the worried look all over him.

We started to run out of bread, milk, and water.

Mr. Williams told everyone what he had heard on the radio in case they hadn't heard.

"They're telling us to get out of town," he said. "All the traffic is going out of town."

When it slowed up a bit in the store, I said I needed to get home. JayEl said he'd walk me.

I laughed. "JayEl, your daddy need you. I don't need no walking home like I is three." JayEl looked strange, like I slapped him or something. So I says, "I come back later if I can."

When I gots home, Mammaloose and Uncle Gilbert were in the kitchen eating.

"Where you been?" she asked.

"I said where." I gave Uncle Gilbert glances.

"I tol' her," he said.

They was eating take-away from somewheres.

"There's plenty you want some," Uncle Gilbert said.

"I ate," I said. That was not a complete and entire truth. I did eat some time that day but had not for a good while now.

I sat at the table with them.

"Are we going to leave town?" I asked.

"Where we gonna go?" Mammaloose said.

"I don't think it matters," I said. "That storm is huge. It could wash us all away."

"The mayor didn't tell us to go," she said. "It'll be fine. You worry too much."

She seemed to be in a good-time mood. I had a wondering if maybe she drinking. But she don't do that. Much. Every once in a while she and Uncle Gilbert share some beers and something else that smells sweet. Not sure what. She get a little silly.

"I think we should leave town," I said to her again.

"We can't afford a motel," she said, "and I doubt that car get us twenty miles down the road anyway."

"It'd get us to Baton Rouge," I said. "They probably have shelters there."

"They gonna open the dome again?" Uncle Gilbert asked. "We could go there if need be."

"We can go to hotel where I work," Mammaloose said, "if we has to leave here."

"They talking about the levees failing," I said. "We're below sea level."

"Why ain't there shelters here where we live?" Uncle Gilbert asked.

"Because we're below sea level," I said. "They'd get flooded. Just like we'll get flooded."

"We'll put everything upstairs tomorrow," Mammaloose said. "Now I'm tired. I'm gonna look at the teevee and then go to bed."

"Shouldn't we get supplies if we're staying here?" I said. "We probably won't have food or water or electricity for a few days."

"Mr. Grant has a boat," Mammaloose said. "He said he'll go make groceries for us anytime. You do the dishes, Ruby Marie."

She never call me Ruby Marie. I look at her. The butterflies in my stomach started flapping so much I open my mouth. Mammaloose is scared. I look right into her eyes and I knows she has fear on her.

"Mammaloose," I said quietly, "you know it's the best thing to leave. So why don't we go?"

Mammaloose pushed her chair back and stood.

"If we leave, they might never let us back. And this house is all I got."

"You've got us," I said. "You've got Uncle Gilbert and me."

She looks at me, then at Uncle Gilbert. "It'll be all right." She walks away. "Gilbert, you fill up that car with gas tomorrow, you hear? Just in case we have to go to the hotel."

"I went around before I picked you up today," he said. "There's lines everywhere."

"I seen you wait in a drive-up daiquiri line for twenty minutes," she said. "You can wait for gas some."

Uncle Gilbert cleared his throat. "You got any money?"

"Ask me tomorrow," Mammaloose said. "I'll get it then."

I watched Uncle Gilbert eat for a minute. I had bad feels, but I didn't know what else to do. I went outside and next door to see Mr. Grant.

He was sitting on his steps.

"How you doin'?" he asked.

I sat next to him.

"Are you leaving?" I asked.

"I got nowhere to go," he said. "I probably go to the dome tomorrow. Bob Connor coming over to help me board up. They leaving first thing. Offered me a ride. Might take it."

"You want to come over and look at teevee at Mammaloose's?" I asked. Mr. Grant didn't have a television.

"No, thank you," he said. "My lady friend coming over later. We'll have a hurricane party of our own."

"Mammaloose says you have a boat?" I said.

He nodded. "I had it for years. You never seen it back there? I had plants in it. I took them out and I'll tie it up to something so the wind don't blow it away." He shrugged. "Never know."

"Come on over you want," I said.

I walked down to the store. Just a few people inside. The cupboards were looking bare. And Mr. Williams and JayEl had the tired looks. JayEl and I went outside and sat up against the building.

"We're leaving in the morning," JayEl said. "We're picking up my auntie and then we're gone. You wanna come?"

"I don't know what we doing," I said. "Mammaloose and Uncle Gilbert acts like nothing happening. The Lady told me not to wait too long."

"Doesn't look like we'll have school on Monday," JayEl said.

I laughed. "That won't be bad."

"When it's all over, let's run around town and see everything," JayEl said. "It could be something."

"Could be bad something. Everything could be different. We might not know it anymore."

JayEl looked around. "All your spots, all your places, gone? Like this place right here."

"Yessir," I said. "This spot right here. The Place Where I First Saw JayEl."

He nodded.

"I was eating a frozen cup and I saw you and dropped it," he said. "You didn't laugh or nothing. You walked right over and picked it up and handed it to me, looked at me like I was supposed to keep eating it."

"And you said, 'Who you?'"

"And you said, 'Ruby Marie Pelletier. I can take you to meet the Rooted People and the Flying People now you here. They make the way better for you.'"

I laughed. "That's right. I forgot. Your daddy had just bought this place. I hadn't been here long myself. You ask me why my parents called me Ruby. 'That a color or a stone?' you asked."

"You said it was because all their children were treasures," he said. "I never heard no body talk like you. And you looked like you had just walked out of the swamp."

"Used to drive Mammaloose crazy that I run around barefoot," I said, "with my hair going every which way. Being barefoot didn't last long—I kept cutting my feet on glass."

"You told me you went barefoot 'cause you wanted your soul to touch the soul of the Earth," he said.

"I did not," I said.

"You did."

"Didn't I say I wanted my skin to touch the skin of the Earth?"

"You said both things. We walked around that day and you showed me all the Rooted People. Then you brought me back here, like you was taking me on a tour."

"Then you held up your little finger," I said.

He nodded. "And I said, 'Friends forever.'"

"And I curls my little finger over your little finger and said, 'Forever friends.'"

We sat silent for a few minutes, listening to the night falling down on us. The wind pushed the litter around in the parking lot. JayEl and I got up and picked it all up and threw it out.

"You want one last frozen cup?" JayEl said.

"If you drop it," I said, "I'll pick it up for ya. Just likes ole times."

CHAPTER 6

Stun Day

I SLEPT likes a baby. Likes a baby who wakes up crying every hour on da hour. Not that I was crying. I just fell to dreaming, then I'd wakes up all sweaty. I went down early. Mammaloose was making eggs and potatoes, sausages, pancakes. Uncle Gilbert sat at the table already eating. The radio on.

"After he's done eating," Mammaloose said, "he gonna get gasoline. You got any money?"

"About five dollars," I said. I pulls it out of the pocket of my jeans and hands it to Uncle Gilbert.

"We're going to the hotel as soon as you come back," Mammaloose said to Uncle Gilbert. "Stop at the Winn-Dixie and get some water if you can. Ruby, you pack clothes for a couple days. And we'll put the good stuff upstairs, just in case."

I nodded. I had the relief feels that Mammaloose

was doing something. We ate together, the three of us, saying no words to one another. After, Uncle Gilbert left. I could hear his old car rattling as it went down the street. I went outside to the Place Where My Vegetables Grow. Soon as I got there Samuel Beckett Sparrow flies down to the wisteria and looks at me.

"What you still doing here?" I asked. "I'm leaving. You best be leaving too. Look, Maya Angelou gone."

Samuel Beckett Sparrow looked at me with forlorn eyes. I scooped up some seeds from the feeder and held my hand out. He hopped from the wisteria to my arm. He looks at me, looks at the seeds, then he picks one up in his beak. He looks at me again.

"Thanks for being my friend," I told him. "I'll see you on the other side of the storm."

He flies away with the seed in his beak. I watch him until he just a speck. I picks up the feeder by the Place Where My Vegetables Grow and the one by the door and I takes them upstairs and puts them in my locker. Mammaloose stayed cooking in the kitchen, setting aside food for us to take. I carries upstairs those things I know Mammaloose likes. Not much.

JayEl and Mr. Williams came over and boarded up our windows. Mammaloose just stood with her hands on her hips and asked them what they up to. Mr. Williams said, "You don't want it, I won't put it up, but I had some extra board. Might as well put it to use."

"Don't see nobody else doing this," Mammaloose said.

"I seen lots of people boarding up yesterday," JayEl said. "Most of them gone now."

Mammaloose puts on him one of her squinty-eyed stares. JayEl looks like he gonna laugh all over hisself, but I gives him a look that reminds him I gots to live with this woman.

"You go ahead then if you want," Mammaloose says; then she goes back in the house.

The mayor comes on the radio and the teevee again to say we all have to gets out of town. JayEl and Mr. Williams comes inside to listen.

"I wish I had better news," the mayor said, "but

we're facing the storm most of us have feared. This is very serious."

Mammaloose just stare at the teevee.

"The first choice of every citizen should be to leave the city," he said.

"Your hotel is still in the city, Mammaloose," I said. "That hurricane is a category five. It could blow this city away. It could drown us all."

"Shut your mouth, Ruby," she said. "Listen. They're opening the dome. If it gets bad, we'll go there." She turned away from the teevee. "Where is Gilbert? Can't take that long to get gasoline."

"They've closed lots of gasoline stations," Mr. Williams said, "and the others have lineups. We can take you all someplace."

"We'll wait for Gilbert," Mammaloose said. "And this neighborhood was fine during Betsy. Just a little flooding."

"This is bigger than Betsy," JayEl said.

Mammaloose ignored him. She always do that. Like anyone who isn't her don't have no things to say that she wants to listen to.

Mr. Williams said, "We can take Ruby with us. She'd be welcome."

JayEl looks at me and nods. I likes that idea just fine.

"I don't know where you going or when you coming back," Mammaloose said. "Ruby is my responsibility. I take care of her just like I always have."

"We're going to Baton Rouge, where my wife is staying with her sister," Mr. Williams said. "I'll give you the phone number."

Mammaloose shook her head. "Where is Gilbert?"

"I better stay here," I said.

"We're going to take Mr. Grant and Miss Sweet Desserts to the Superdome," Mr. Williams said. "Then we'll pick up my sister. You want us to stop back?"

"We'll be fine," Mammaloose said.

JayEl and Mr. Williams both have the worried looks. I followed them out to their car. Mr. Williams leaned into the car and pulled out an ax and several bottles of water.

"Just in case," he said as he holds them out to me.

I took them. "Thank you."

Mr. Williams put his arms around me and gave me a big ole hug.

"You be awright," he said.

He let me go and walked over to Mr. Grant's house. JayEl and I looked at each other.

"You be full of cares," I said. "Those roads ain't gonna be fun."

"I bought a little camera," he said. "I'll take pictures and show them to you later."

"You do that," I said.

"Maybe it won't be so bad," he said.

I held out my little finger. He curled his little finger around mine.

"When did you get so big?" I asked.

"When did you get so little?"

We kept our fingers together for a moment.

"Forever friends," I said.

"Friends forever," he said.

Then we pulled our hands away from each other.

Mr. Williams came back to the car alone.

"Where's Mr. Grant?" I asked.

"He said he is gonna wait for his lady friend," Mr. Williams said. "Then they're going together."

JayEl and Mr. Williams got into the car. Then they drove away. I watched until they stopped at Miss Sweet Desserts's, then I went inside.

Sometimes you're not sure how things happen the way they do—you know what I mean? That's what happened Sunday while we waited for da storm. I knows the wind shook the house every once in a while. I works on my homework. The teevee talks and talks about the hurricane. After we eat lunch, Mammaloose start calling around to ask if anyone had seen Uncle Gilbert. She angry and scared at the same time. Someone hurt him? He drunk somewhere? Car finally break down? She asks the air these questions. The air didn't answer, and Uncle Gilbert didn't come.

Other people called. I hear Mammaloose mad at someone: "We're gonna leave! Ain't none of your business!" She slams down the phone. Later they calls again. She talks quieter and after tells me there are busybodies everywhere.

I plays with the radi, so I can hears what they all saying. One man called Robinette says to us, "You're going to think I'm stone-cold crazy. But the birds are gone. I know the powers that be say not to panic. I'm telling you, panic, worry, run. The birds are gone. Get out of town! Now! Don't stay! Leave! Save yourself while you can. Go . . . go . . . go!"

"Turn that off," Mammaloose said.

"Mammaloose," I finally said, "we got to leave here. Let's go to the dome or to the hotel. Maybe we can get a taxicab."

"You go ahead and call," Mammaloose said. "I gave Gilbert all my cash, but maybe they'll take us anyway."

I called and tried to get someone to take us to the dome. Nobody could come. They was either all busy or didn't answer. Then Mammaloose called people from work.

"We could walk to the dome," I says. "It'd take a while, but we should get there before the storm."

In my memory I could see Samuel Beckett Sparrow looking at me. He had wanted me to leave, just like Ruby Butterfly and the Rooted People had wanted me to leave.

"Mammaloose?"

She didn't answer.

I went outside and stood in the street. It was so quiet. Full of peace, it seemed. No one around I could see. Just me and the rain and the sense of strange that comes before every storm—you know what I mean? Like something is gonna happen. May not be something big. May not be something small. But things are changing.

I went back into the house. I took the water up the stairs to my room. I brought some food too, and the ax Mr. Williams gave us. I asked Mammaloose she want to sleep on my bed. I sleep on the floor, I say. She stop talking much and stayed downstairs. I put a flashlight by her bed. Then I sit upstairs and listen to the radio until I fall asleep.

I never heard Uncle Gilbert come home. I never heard nothing.

CHAPTER 7

Monster Day

I CAN'T tell you for certain when the electricity went out or when the storm came knocking on Mammaloose's door. I only know I woke up and I felt almost relaxed, like some kind of hum I'd been hearing my whole life long had stopped. And the house was shaking and rattling. I didn't know if I had slept through the whole night or if I'd slept an hour. I tried the light, and it didn't work. The windows were boarded up so I didn't know if it was night or day. I could hear the wind. It didn't sound like the air or the wind I knew. It sounded desperate and loud.

It was so dark that I was happy I was not small anymore or I would have felt the bad feels. I stayed in the bed all alone for some whiles. Don't know how long. Then I decided to see how Mammaloose and Uncle Gilbert was. I made my hands my eyes as I felt my way down the stairs.

"Mammaloose?" I whispered when I got to the living room. "Uncle Gilbert?"

Just then I felt something tickling the sides of my feet. Like someone was running a feather along both of them. I realized it was nothing from the Flying People. It was water.

"Mammaloose!" I yells. I try to hurry into her room, but it is so dark. "Mammaloose! There's water in the house!"

"What?"

I gets into her room and grab for the flashlight I knows is on her nightstand.

"What's happening?"

"It's flooding," I said. I switched on the flashlight and shined the light on Mammaloose. Uncle Gilbert was not in the bed with her.

"We've got to get upstairs," I said. "It's flooding."

I shined the light on the floor. The water was up to my ankles. Just then we heard a kind of explosion. We both jumped. I heard a roar of something. Wind or water or da end of da earth.

Mammaloose grabbed my arm and we sloshed

through the water. A bit of light come through the burst door, where water was pouring through. It was near up to my knees. I pulled Mammaloose to the stairs. It was hard walking through the water. Like in a dream when you tries to run but you can't. It was like that. Something floating in the water knocked into Mammaloose. I grabbed her and dropped the flashlight in the water. I reach for it, but the light went out.

We in darkness.

I pull on Mammaloose and she pull on me and we somehow gets to the stairs and go up. I looked back down the stairs and the little bit of light from the open front door shows the water following us.

I never heard nothing so loud as this storm. And it was so dark and loud and I was shivering inside because I never in my life felt as alone as I did that moment, like nothing else existed anywhere but this whirlwind of sound and it wasn't nothing personal but I was gonna be sucked away and be a part of the noise and the wet darkness forever. Just then Mammaloose grabbed my arm. She saying something, maybe, but I can't see or hear her. I get turned around, but she pull me closer.

"We got to get into the attic," she says.

I pull away and go into my room and find the water bottles and the bag of beignets and the bread Mr. Lagniappe made for me. Then I go back to Mammaloose. This takes only a few seconds in the roar and the darkness, but Mammaloose screams in my ear, "Don't leave me again!" I hold onto her sleeve as she goes to the end of the hall and pulls the string to the attic door. The steps fall down—I can't see them but I feel them. Mammaloose goes up first. I follow her and put the water and food on the attic floor. Then I remember the ax.

I yell to Mammaloose that I'm going for the ax. Before she can say anything, I step down the ladder again. I keep my hands against the wall until I come to my room. Then I feel the tickle again, only this time it's not so slow. This time I know it's water. I tries to make a picture in my head of exactly where I put the ax. On the floor by the bed? I reach down. It's all water. It's lapping at my feet like I am at some kind of sandy beach. Only the tide is coming in, way in. And the roar keeps on. Roar is the wrong word. It's different than that. Like a train and a whistle and white noise all at once. Where is the ax? The water is around my ankles now, like chilly hands gonna take me under.

The three-legged chair. Yes! I feel around for it. It is still standing! I grabs the handle of the ax and then tries to run through the water. But it pushes me like some big bully in school. I can't push back. Can't use the ax. Just has to keep going.

Outside in the hall. Down the hall. My fingers my eyes. Where is the ladder? Where is the ladder? The water is getting to my knees.

Where is the ladder?

I want to scream.

Then suddenly I see the light. Shining down onto the ladder. I grab the ladder and go up it. Mamma-loose holding a flashlight on me. I get in the attic, and she pulls the door shut. For a moment it seems like silence. My ears pulse with echoes of the noise.

"That switch here hardly ever works," Mammaloose yelled. "So I put a flashlight up here long ago."

The house was shaking. Or moving. Like it was
just about to become part of the Flying People.

Some light came through the small attic window
Mr. Williams and JayEl hadn't boarded up. Suddenly
the glass shattered. I screamed. Mammaloose
screamed. Or the wind did. Heard a dull boom outside. The house shuddered. Something hit it? Rain
came through the broken window. Mammaloose and
I crawled away from it.

I picked up the flashlight and shined the light
around the tiny attic. I never came up here. Mammaloose said I can't, so I never did. Now I gots up and
went to a box and opened it. Papers. Another box.
Clothes. I grabbed up a bunch of clothes and then
stuffed them into the window. I was as surprised as
anyone in that attic that the clothes stopped the better part of the whining and the wind from getting
in — and they stayed in place.

Mammaloose shut off the flashlight.

"In case we need it later," she said. I could hear the shivers in her voice.

"You cold?" I asked. "I can look through those boxes for something warm."

"I don't want you looking through my things," Mammaloose said.

"Your things are about to go floating away," I said, "so I wouldn't be so concerned about them right now."

The house shivered and shook and moaned.

I hoped everyone was safe and full of cares.

The Place Where My Vegetables Grow was drowned. Was my Garden of Neighbors drowned too?

I got the flashlight and lifted the attic door and shined the light on the water. It looked like we was living above a lake. I dropped the ladder down to see how far up the water came. Below the third rung. It had eight. I lifted the ladder and closed the door again.

"It's not pouring in," I said, "but it might be rising still."

"How high can it go?"

"I don't know," I said. "How far below sea level are we here?"

"Now, why would I know that?"

"Because we live in a bowl," I said. "We live in a place that wants to be a lake. We should know."

"You don't know," Mammaloose said.

"That's right," I said. "I'm just as ignorant as . . ."

I stopped myself.

The house groaned. It was loud and it lasted a long time and I squeezed my eyes shut, waiting for it all to blow up around us.

But it didn't.

I heard Mammaloose shivering. I turned the light on the boxes again, dug around, and came up with an old sweater of Uncle Gilbert's. What she hanging on to that for?

I brought it to her and she put it on.

"You eat something too," I said. "I made those beignets myself. You can try Mr. Lagniappe's bread if you don't want the beignets."

I turned off the light again, but I could hear

Mammaloose opening the bag. My eyes adjusted to the almost-darkness, but my ears and body could not get used to the noise or the shuddering of the house. It was like something was outside trying to get to us and it would only stop once the house blew apart and we was in the water.

"You think Gilbert alive?" Mammaloose asked. She handed the bag to me.

"He alive."

"I wonder how long this will last," she said. "Whole street must be under water. This beignet is good. What is that? Chili powder?"

"And chocolate," I said. No one had guessed before.

I opened the bag and took out a beignet. I bit into it. Could just barely taste the cocoa. Seemed strange to have that on my tongue up in this place.

We sat likes this for what seemed like many days. The house creaked and whined, and the wind it did just scream and howl at us like some crazy hurt thing.

Then the house began groaning again, and it did

not stop. This time it was so loud. You ever see those movies when a ship is about to go under the water for all time? That's what it sounded like. I hears Mammaloose's scream. Think I'll remember that for all time. Her scream was full of so much wrong. So much sad. So much at the end of everything.

Seemed her scream was the last bit of air or something the storm needed. A piece of the roof blew off, and we was looking at daylight. Only it wasn't daylight. It was rain and wind fighting each other to see who could hurt us worse: the sound in my ears or the rain hitting me like little pieces of glass. I reached for Mammaloose. I didn't want the wind to take her away. She reached for me.

One, two, three — the rest of the roof flew away. Mammaloose and I held on to each other and moved together to a corner. Somehow that felt safer. Our house was in the middle of a sea. I tell you, it was a sea beyond my wildest imagine! It was gray and choppy, and the tops of some houses grew out of this new sea. Somehow our house had floated out into the Gulf of Mexico. No, no, that couldn't be it. The Gulf must have come to us. Or the lake. Or something. And the wind howled. It felt so alive. I was afraid it was going to reach in and pick us up. Mammaloose and I ducked our heads as pieces of houses and buildings and trees flew over us. The house stopped creaking, as if relieved of some burden now that the roof was gone. I put my hands over my ears. Mammaloose screamed, "No, no, don't leave me!" So I put my arms around her again and we held each other tight. Nothing else to do. We'd either be drowned or blown away or we'd get through it. Just hold each other. The Place Where My Vegetables Grow was gone. Mr. Grant's house was almost all under water. His boat was still tied to the tree and it bobbed in the water, right side up. I couldn't see the Corner of Happiness Store from here. Nearly every house was drowned.

I don't know how long this went on. I don't know how long we sat on the floor of that attic hoping the water wouldn't rise no more and the wind wouldn't see us there shivering and take us away. It seemed like it was longer than I had even been on the earth.

Stuff kept blowing away from our attic. Like the storm was reaching down and searching for something. Didn't find it, so it tossed what it did find into the water. Mammaloose cried and shivered and began whispering in my ear. For a long time I didn't listen. The wind was too loud. I thought she was praying. Or something. But then I began to hear her words more distinctly. She was saying something about being sorry. Sorry she'd been so mean to me. Sorry she hadn't been better. She wanted to be nice. I reminded her of my momma. It broke her heart when my momma left to marry my daddy. It broke her heart when my momma started doing those drugs.

"She left you all and came back here and I was glad until I see she doing the drugs again like she had when she was a girl. Your daddy promised to keep her straight but he didn't do no better than I did. I told your daddy that he had taken a daughter from me, so he owed me one. A devil's bargain. He and your momma got into some trouble. She robbed a store while he was in the car. She was running from the law. She was. I coulda turned her in. Maybe that would have turned her around. But I couldn't do it. He should have known I couldn't do it. She disappeared. I told him, you give me one of those girls or I'll turn you in. You and her. Then I get all three. He did it. He gave me you. I made him promise to go away and never contact you or I'd turn them in. For the robbery and abandonment. I was so angry. I was so angry about my Emmy. She came back here sometimes. Never straight. I couldn't let her see you. She never could be out in the swamp for long. It was just too much for her."

She said this over and over, like a record, until I began to hears it and sees it in my head.

"What? What you saying?"

I tried to push her away from me, but she held on tight.

"Mammaloose!" I pulled away. "Are you saying I did live in the bayou? I do have sisters?"

Mammaloose's face looked like putty, like it had no shape.

"What about my sisters? Where are they? When did momma and daddy die?"

She looked at me. The sea moved around us, like water in a pot about to boil. Mammaloose stared at me and I could see the truth.

It felt like my head cracked open.

My daddy and momma hadn't died in a car accident. *They were alive.* And my sisters were real. My sisters were alive. Everyone was alive.

And Mammaloose had kept them from me my whole life.

The storm spun around us for a long time. Seemed like every few minutes the house shivered or moved or did something that made me think it was gonna disappear and drown us. Mammaloose huddled in the corner. I sat right next to her, but I couldn't look at her. I tried not to think on what she told me. Maybe it was all a lie. Maybe she gone crazy.

We stayed like this a long while. We soaked to the bone, cold, full of fears, until finally the wind and the rain got less and it seemed likes we weren't gonna blow away. The wind hadn't taken the bags of beignets and Mr. Lagniappe's bread or the water, so

I ate and drank some of it. I gave some to Mamma-loose too. She came out of her stupor somewhat to look around. Wasn't much left we knows.

"They'll come for us," Mammaloose said. "They'll come now."

So we waited. Once I lifted the door and looked down. The water had risen some but not much. Maybe we be all right until help came or the water went away. Unless the water was trapped. Unless all of the city now that lake.

We was lucky to be alive, Mammaloose and me, and I wanted to be happy about that.

When we could hear each other talk, I said to Mammaloose, "Was all that you told to me true?"

She looked me straight in the eye, like she got nothing to be sorry for.

"Yes, it's all true," she said. "And I did you a favor. Your daddy was so poor he couldn't feed you all. You had a roof over your head for all your life."

I looked up at the sky. We didn't have a roof no more. Almost made me laugh. Felt kind of silly. Like adrenaline pumping all through me for hours thinking I was gonna die and now I was alive, I was alive, and I was still pumping.

"You've got a scholarship for college," she said. "You wouldn't have had any of that."

"But why did you lie to me? Why did you make me think I was crazy for remembering all those things about the swamp and my sisters?"

"I thought it would be better for you to forget the whole thing," she said. "I've forgotten half my life. It's better that way."

"You had no right to make that decision!"

"Your daddy agreed with it," she said. "You didn't see him coming around all the time you were growing up."

"So where are they?"

"I don't know," Mammaloose said. "Your momma was around for a while. She lived here on the block for a time. You took care of her yard."

"Miss Emmy? That was my mother?"

Another lie.

"Why didn't she tell me?"

"Same reason," Mammaloose said. "I told her I'd

turn her in if she said anything to you. They was still looking for her for that robbery."

"They can't still be looking for her!" I said. "Do I have two sisters? Are they called Opal and Pearl?"

Mammaloose looked out over the New Sea. "I wonder if Gilbert is awright."

"Mawmaw!"

She looked at me. She hate when I calls her that.

"Yes, you have two sisters. I don't know where none of them is! I don't know if they even still alive."

"Why wouldn't they be alive? Were they sick?"

"I just mean I don't know. So there's nothing you can do about it."

I shook my head. JayEl had been right. All this time I was too nice to her.

"This storm took away everything," Mammaloose said.

I wanted to say to her that she took everything away from me. I wanted to tells her I'm gonna rename her Hurricane Mammaloose, category 10. But I was so tired and wet and afraid that I think maybe this wasn't the best time for an argument. I didn't see no bodies coming to help. I saw lots of things in the water. Things churned up by the waves. A dead dog. A piece of a couch. Toys. Clothes. Looks like there is wires everywhere. A lampshade. Most stuff I can't tells what it is. The Cooper house, where my momma used to live, is above water too, but it looks like it moved closer or off or something. It was all different. We sees a man swim by. He didn't look up at us or nothing when we calls out. We didn't know him. Didn't know where he swimming to, but he just keep going.

"I lived in the swamp like I thought?" I asked Mammaloose.

"I don't want to talk about this," Mammaloose said.

"You told me the truth," I said. "Now I want to hear all about my family."

"I'm your family," she said. "Uncle Gilbert is your family."

"Uncle Gilbert is no family," I said. "He just this man."

I had the bad feels. I had the mean feels.

"He's been a better father to you than your own," she said.

"He's never been like a father," I said. "He was drunk for years. He used to try to give me beer when I was small, did you know that?"

"But he was here."

"My daddy wasn't here because you took me away from him," I said. "Why'd you do that? Why did you want me?"

"Your momma was taking drugs and she couldn't take care of any of you," she said. "Your daddy was poor as dirt, and your sisters running around like they was wild. You was young enough, I figured I could help you. He let you go easy enough. He must have thought so too."

I looks away from her. I can see the ruin of the world. Maybe my daddy let go of me because I was Ruby. Because I was crazy Ruby.

"Your daddy loved you," Mammaloose said, as though she be reading my mind. "There was nothing wrong with you that he let you go."

"Even though you've told me there was some-thing wrong with me my whole life!"

"Well, Ruby, you are different from anyone else I know," Mammaloose said. "That ain't bad, but it worried me. Your momma was different too, and I loved her and gave her everything she wanted and she got messed up on drugs. I thought I'd raise you up different. Maybe things would turn out better for you."

"You was mean," I said. "I can see you maybe thinking my daddy and momma have some trouble. Maybe. But why you take my sisters away from me? Do you know how many nights I lay in bed thinking about them, imagining what my life would be like if I was with them?"

"Ruby's imagine," she said.

"Only it could have been true!"

Mammaloose shook her head. "I did the best I could. Maybe it was wrong. But I meant it to be right."

"You meant it to be right? You should have shown me some love and kindness then."

"Showed you love and kindness? I fed you. I clothed you. I wiped your knees when you scraped them. I made sure you went to school. I watched what kind of friends you had. Isn't that love and kindness? I kept you on the straight and narrow, Ruby Marie. Look what you've grown up into! You're going to college. You'll have a life different from mine, different from your momma's. You'll be someone!"

"I already am someone," I said.

"I know it," Mammaloose said. "I always knew it. I just didn't want you to get lost, like your momma. Or like me."

I looked at her. She looked out at the ruin. Then we had quiet between us.

We sat there in the roofless attic for a long time, listening and watching the sky for help. We watched the water to see if it would go down. It didn't. Every once in a while I thought I hears a helicopter. Mammaloose would perk up then, saying we'd be rescued anytime now. Nobody came. We couldn't hear any other people. Maybe the whole city dead and gone 'cept us—and the swimming man. It got dark and Mammaloose started crying. That almost worse to hear than the wind. My ears still ringing from the wind, like I was constantly listening to a seashell. The ocean in my ears. Or the New Sea in my ears. I didn't like the darkness. I could hear a dog howling from far away, or moaning. It so sad and lonely. That the only sound. Except maybe a pop now and again. Not sure if it gunfire or electricity or what. The night stank of gasoline and sewage.

"Why don't they come for us?" Mammaloose asked.

"Maybe the whole world is like this," I said. "Maybe there are no bodies left to come for us."

CHAPTER 8

Stews Day

IT WAS a long night. I tell you, I thoughts all kinds of things. I did an entire imagine of what my life would have been like if Mammaloose hadn't taken me from my daddy. Or if he hadn't given me up. And why? Why would he do that? Was he saving himself or his wife? My momma. And where was she now? Where were they all? Why didn't they try to come see me? They older now. Where were they?

I hears and smells all manner of bad things. Mammaloose and I don't talk much until it gets dark. Then we start talking about food. When we get down from here, we make ourselves a fine feast, we say. We stay close to each other, so we knows where we is, even in the dark, even though I had the mad feels about her.

Sometime I lay on the attic floor and looks up at the sky. It is so dark that I can see the stars. I can see the Milky Way, just likes when I lives in the swamp. I have beautiful feels just then, my back against the wood, looking up at all those stars and suns and galaxies. I think I falls to sleep listening to the stars sing to me. Or else I dreams this.

I wakes up and hears dogs barking and howling. Still dark. Someone screaming. I stands up and look. Was that a circle of light from a rescue helicopter in the distance? Nothing happens where we is, no one comes. Mammaloose cries. I ask her if she okay, but she just breathes. She is crying in her sleep.

When dawn comes, the water seems the same height, maybe more of it, but I is glad to have the light, to know whether I'm gonna drown or not. I stand up and look in the distant and I can see other people on the roofs and porches blocks away. I wave. Some wave back. Mammaloose sitting up eating and drinking the water. Our supplies are not going to last long.

"I think I should go get help," I said. "No one knows we're here."

"How you gonna do that?"

I look over at Mr. Grant's house. That little boat still there, oars stuck in the sides of it. Mammaloose looks at what I is looking at.

"How you gonna get down there?" she asked.

"I could swim," I said. "Like that man yesterday."

"That water is filthy," Mammaloose said. "And you can't swim."

"You don't still have the plastic blow=up swimming pool, do you? I could blow it up and paddle my way over to the boat."

"It's probably in with the box of your old toys," Mammaloose said. "It was under those eaves."

I turned around. A couple of the boxes were still pushed up under the eaves. I pulled them out and dug around. I found an old doll of mine. "I wonder where she got to."

"You were getting too old for dolls," Mammaloose said.

A couple of books. Box of dominoes. And the old pool filling up the bottom of the box.

I pulled it out and looked for the plug. Then I began blowing my air into it.

"You get in that and it'll sink," Mammaloose said. "It wasn't made to float."

She was right. I kept blowing anyway.

"I'll try it on the second floor. That's only about a foot of water, so even if I sink I'll be all right."

When the round sides bulged out I closed the plug. Then I pushed the pool through the attic door and followed it down. I kept a hold of the side as I dropped it into the water. Then I put my foot in the floor of the swimming pool. I tried to put my weight in it. The pool folded right up. Mammaloose was right. It wouldn't do anything but help drown me. I left it in the water and went back up to the attic. I looked down at Mr. Grant's boat. It was near the back of our house, almost resting against it.

"I could jump into it," I said.

"That's ten feet," Mammaloose said. "If not more. You could miss the boat and go into the water. Or you could knock it over."

"No. That's about six feet. I could do that."

I had no ideas at all if I could do that. I was scared of doing it. But I was more scared of staying here. The smell was hurting my lungs. I saw dead dogs and cats float by. Some birds: I only knew they was birds 'cause I saw the feathers and the wings. If I stayed here long enough would I see everything dead in the world float by? I did not want that in my imagine. I had to go and find us some help.

"I'm doing it," I said.

"How will you get back up?"

"I'll get help, and then we'll figure how to get you down."

"You're going to leave me here and never come back."

I looked at Mammaloose. Had she done gone crazy?

"That's what Gilbert did."

"I don't think so," I said. "I'm coming back."

"Don't go." I never seen Mammaloose look so afraid. She looked little now, all tired and worn and wet. Why was I full of fears for her all those years?

"I'm going," I said. "I'll be back."

I am not sure how I did what came next. I climbed out of the attic and onto what was left of that part of the roof. I sees the roof of the back porch is still on and just above the water. The boat is right next to it. I have glad feels—or something like it—to see this. I be full of cares as I walks and crawls and hangs down until I'm on the back porch roof.

The boat is bobbing in the water only a couple feet away, but it is still out of reach. I grab a broken branch floating in the water and I use it to pull the boat to me. Then it took some maneuvering—and me almost going into the water once or twice—before I gets into the boat. Once I'm there, I try the oars. They work. The boat rocked gently in the New Sea. Now I needed to get the rope off. That rope lasted through a hurricane. How was I gonna break it?

I didn't need to. The knot was in a kind of loop. When I pulled the end, it easily came undone.

Just like Mammaloose. She was crying and carrying on.

"Don't leave me!"

"Mammaloose, I am going for help."

I was gonna have to ask Mr. Grant how he did that knot when I saw him again.

"But it all looks different," Mammaloose said. "How you gonna find your way back?"

"That old oak and the gum tree are still standing. I'll know them."

"They look like any other tree."

"I know the Rooted People," I said. "I know the marks of the land."

"There is no land!" Mammaloose said.

"I'll be back. I promise."

"I know where your sisters are," she yelled. "You come back for me and I'll tell you!"

I looks up at her. What was she saying? Was she trying to *bribe* me? What was wrong with her?

"Who are you?" I asked. "You can't be the woman who raised me. She could not be that mean or that awful. She could not believe she would have to say something like that for me to come back. She would know I keep my promises."

I shook my head. Then I started to row. For a minute or so, I was rowing around in circles. But I got it all figured out. I started rowing away from the house. I didn't look back at Mammaloose, but I hears her call out, "You be careful. I don't see you again, you know I did my best. You take care of yourself."

I says to myself, "Your best wasn't good enough."

But even as I said it, it felt mean. I put a hand up and waved. I figured I'd go toward Vieux Carre. It didn't usually flood much, so I could find someone there to help us. As I rowed down my street, things hit the bottom of the boat, scraping it, making it shudder. I has to say that I felt full of fear, but I was glad to be in this boat. I was glad to be away from Mammaloose. I was glad to be doing something to get myself right. I felt like I could row right to the bayou where I had left my family in the way-back time.

I rowed around those things that was floating, went under wires and such. After a while I could see the corner store up the river road a bit. I couldn't see the Place Where I First Met JayEl. Couldn't see the RTA sign JayEl was always leaning against. It all underwater. I should go on up close so I could tell him what it was like — once I saw him again. How would I ever find him? He was someplace up in Baton Rouge. I was down here. Our whole world drowned. What if we never saw each other again? What if I never got to tell him about Opal and Pearl?

As I rowed near the store, I saw that the whole second-story looked all right. Maybe they didn't lose everything. It still sad, though. I wondered if they had any idea up there in Baton Rouge how bad it was down here.

Then I heard shouts. I looked at the upstairs window in the store and there is JayEl, leaning out, calling my name.

"What you doing here?" I said as I rowed toward him. "You're supposed to be safe!"

"I'll tell you later," he said. "Dad's here too. Where's Mammaloose and Gilbert?"

"Uncle Gilbert never came home," I said. "And Mammaloose is in the attic. Our roof got blown off. I told her I'd get some help. Do you have a radio or anything? You heard what's happening? Is it flooded just here?"

"No, it's all over the city," JayEl said. "It's real bad, Ruby."

Mr. Williams come out the back porch.

"Ruby," he said. "I am sorry to see you're still here. You awright?"

"Mammaloose is in the attic," I said. "The roof is off. I was gonna try and get someplace where I could find someone to help. She can't come down on her own. I could hardly do it."

"We'll help you find someone to get her down," Mr. Williams said. "We all need to get some help."

I rowed to the balcony. JayEl dropped down a couple of bags of food and water, and then he and Mr. Williams climbed down into the boat.

We took turns rowing the boat through the New Sea. Sometimes it was easy sailing going around the different Gardens of Neighbors, but sometimes there was so much rubbish and junk clogging everything. Put on the imagines that you have a basket full of toys. Now mix them all up and smash them up. Then throw them outs on the ground and fills your world up with water and pour oil or gasoline or chemicals all over the top of it. That's what we rowed through. And the stink was terrible. We see people on roofs and balconies. They wave to us and tell us their names.

"We going for help!" I called.

We pass people floating on boards and doors and pieces of styrofoam, trying to get here or there. Some places they walking, pulling something through the water that carries their child or dog. Most everyone looked dazed, like they not sure all this is real. We sees lots of people we could help but we don't have the ways. Strange to see the world so different. Some trees gone too. Some just rising up out of the mess. Nothing seemed organized. But not wild. Wild is organized in its own way. This was just crazy-looking.

We row around our city until we come near the Crossroads. I see it just on shore. That's what it feels like, when I see it ain't flooded, like we're in the New Sea and they on shore. Just when I see it, another boat comes up along beside us. This one bigger, and Mr. Lagniappe is driving it.

I am so happy to see him — and sad, too. I hoped he be long gone. He looks so surprised to see me. His face is full of the shocks.

"Ruby girl," he said. "I thought you were gone days ago."

"Uncle Gilbert never come home," I said, "and he had the car."

"I wish you'd called," he said. "I could have helped."

"I thought you were gone," I said. "Your daughters must be worried."

"I kept driving people out of the city or to the dome, and then it got late and I was out of gas. I stayed here with the Lady. She got some flooding, but just up to the steps. She pretty dry otherwise. No electricity or water, of course. I've been going out all day getting people."

"Where'd you get the boat?" JayEl asked.

"I borrowed it," he said. "Didn't seem like nothing was happening otherwise."

"I borrowed this one too," I said.

The Lady came out the door of the Crossroads.

We was just about ten feet away. She waved. I waved back. I wanted to jump in the water and run to her. I was full of glad feels to see her.

"Mr. Lagniappe, this here is Mr. Benjamin Williams, and you know JayEl."

The men reached across the water to shake hands.

"Callaway Lanier," he said, "but Ruby calls me Mr. Lagniappe."

"I've been hearing stories about you for years," Mr. Williams said. "Ruby's grandmother is trapped in their house, in the attic. The roof blew off. Can you take me to her?"

"Sure."

"Jacob," Mr. Williams said, "you can stay here with Ruby and the Lady."

"How are you gonna get her out of that attic?" I asked.

"I don't know," Mr. Lagniappe said. "Maybe we can get the Coast Guard to come. We've been working together all morning. They show me where to go and I show them. And Fish and Wildlife is out too, in flatbottom boats. They'll have ideas."

Mr. Williams rowed closer to Mr. Lagniappe's boat, and then he climbed into it.

"I'll bring Mammaloose back here," Mr. Williams said. "Try to get a hold of your mother if you can, Jacob."

I started to say I should go with them. Mammaloose would probably likes to see me there, to knows I did not desert her. But I thinks no, they can do it better without me in the way. Plus, I had the bad feels about Mammaloose still. I knows it looks like the end of the world where we was and I shouldn't be mad. But what if my daddy and momma and sisters were here during the storm? What if they in one of those houses that got drowned? What if they lost or hurt somewheres and I never gets to know them because Mammaloose was mean?

Mr. Lagniappe slowly steered the boat through the debris, away from us. I rowed Mr. Grant's boat to the steps of the Crossroads. JayEl jumped out and pulled the boat closer to the building and tied it to the railing. I got out, and the Lady put her arms around me.

"*Cher!* I'm so glad you're safe!" she said. "This is JayEl, no? JayEl, take that boat around back so it doesn't get stolen. We may need it later. Then come in and I will feed you."

The Lady turned me around and together we walked through the store and into the back, where the candles still burned. We went through the back door and outside again. Her garden area was not flooded, and it was filled with people who were eating and talking, people who looked like they had just been plucked off of rooftops or out of the water. Someone was stirring a pot of something over a propane or kerosene stove. I could smell the food from across the yard. Good to smell something besides gasoline and sewage. JayEl came and stood next to me.

"Wow," he said. "This is something."

"It is good to be prepared," the Lady said. "Now go eat."

JayEl and I sat next to each other on the step after we each got a bowl of gumbo and a slab of bread.

The Lady gave us each a bottle of water and told us to drink.

We ate in silence for a while. The whole of the world was throbbing. Even though people talked, it was still quiet. We heard a helicopter nows and then.

"How come you stayed?" I asked.

"We didn't mean to," JayEl said. "After we drove Lionel and Miss Sweet Desserts to the Superdome, we went to get my aunt, but she had already left. A bunch of people in that neighborhood wanted a ride, so we took them to the dome. We kept picking up people who needed a ride. By the time we tried to get out of town, it was a mess. I got worried about you, so we came back, but nobody answered the door, so I thought you'd left. Then it got late, and then it was too late. I know it's stupid. My mom is gonna kill my dad."

"You came back for me?" I asked. "JayEl."

"I knew your grandma would keep you there to drown," he said.

"She's not some evil thing trying to hurt me," I said.

"I wonder," he said.

I chewed on my bread. I did not feel likes getting into my whole life story.

Then other people began coming to the Crossroads. They wet and tired and crying. The Lady had all kinds of people out in the water and around the city finding those that needed help and then bringing them back to the store or dropping them off somewhere they could get help—or where they thought they could get help. I saw boys I figured were gangsters helping out. JayEl and I help the Lady feed the people and get them dry.

I asked the Lady, "Is it like this all over the city?"

"Yes, *cher*. The flooding is very bad. I hear there are thousands of people at the dome and they can't go anywhere. Water's comin' up. No one coming that we can see. We need to take care of ourselves."

"We've got Mr. Grant's boat," JayEl said. "We could go out and get some people."

"It's too dangerous for you to be out by yourselves," she said. "Last night we were robbed. A group of men came for our jewelry and money. I looked at them and said, 'Where do you think you is? We don't have nothing like that. You is welcome to join us for dinner.' Some boys left this morning to go to the dome and tell someone that people need help out here. And we've got some protection for tonight, I think. Revel!" She calls out and motions to a man across the yard. He comes over. "You need some help going out again to rescue people? This here is JayEl and Ruby. They're offering to help if you think it's safe."

"Nothing safe about it," Revel said. He grinned. His front teeth were partially silver. He looked like an old swamp rat from the way-back time. "But I could use the help. I was just about to go out again. I got Chris and his boys watching the boat fer me. Come on, kids, let's rock 'n' roll. Good morning, Vietnam!"

I looks at the Lady. She nods, like it all right.

"Tell my daddy where we are," JayEl said.

"You find any fresh water, bring it back," the

Lady said. "And take this water for yourselves." She hands us a couple bottles of water each.

We went out front with Revel. Three men with rifles sat on the steps near the boat, which was a kind of raft with an engine, like what Mr. Lagniappe had.

JayEl and I got into the boat behind Revel and we went into the strange waters again. The day was so hot and humid and stinky that it was hard to breathe. We couldn't go fast because there was so much debris and tangled wires. We went to the first building we saw with people on it. We helped one old man and woman, tiny and frail, step off their porch into our boat. They had a little dog about the size of a rat. He came too. We took them to the Lady. Next we got a family: a mother and her three tiny children. The mother couldn't stop crying. The babies just look at her and us. I about start crying then too. The babies didn't hardly have any clothes on them.

I held the youngest one on my lap close to me and said, "I'm sorry, dawlin'. I loves you, I loves you, I loves you." The baby rested her head on my shoulder.

After a while, I gots used to my nose and lungs burning. I felt dizzy and tired and hungry, but the people waving to us and waiting for help was more tired. And some of them looked like they sick. I never seen people look like such. All the bodies the same: wrecked.

No one seemed all panicky like I would have been expecting at the ends of the world. They seemed tired—and not all in their eyes, like long-goners. When I sees they not in their eyes, I put my arms around them if they little—maybe I holds their hand if they big—and I says, "I'm sorry. I'm sorry. I loves you, I loves you, I loves you."

Most don't want to let go of me—and I feels the same—but the Lady takes them and then we goes out again. Revel doesn't talk much, but he can handle the boat, and he does just fine. Sometimes he says to the newcomers to our boat, "Welcome to the end of the world, ladies and germs."

I watched for Mr. Lagniappe and Mr. Williams and Mammaloose, but I didn't see them.

We saw other people helping too. People being helped off roofs and balconies and tops of cars. Boats and makeshift boats wound their way through the New Sea with us. Once we got stuck in some debris and this big ole man come walking right up to us and pushed the boat out. He didn't say one word, just did it, then keeps on walking through the water. Lots of people and pets needed help. We heard the helicopters and saw one close once.

We don't take everyone back to the Lady. Some of them that young and strong and be in their eyes, they tell us just takes them to dry land and they figure it out from there. So we drop them where the water isn't too deep and they walk the rest of the way.

We pass by many things in the New Sea that I thinks I never seen. So many things once living and now dead wrapped in wires and cords. I seen a cow all bloated up. Wonders about where the cow come from, but not for long. It too sad seeing it in the water likes that. We sees us dead birds and dogs and cats and animals we don't recognize. It all so sad. We saw dead people too. It hard to see all the dead, but those be the hardest. They floating or stuck. I don't want to have them in my imagines. I is so sorry they gone. I had to be sick to my stomach then. JayEl put his hand on my back to help me. Later I did the same for him.

I have tears running down my face all day. I have the wondering about hows I can keep doing this. JayEl and I sits in the boat with Revel for a minute, just resting and drinking some water, when it seems likes something bursts or blossoms or breaks open: The air is suddenly filled with dragonflies. They is everywhere. (I knows people here calls them mosquito hawks, but I likes the word *dragonfly* better.) Their shiny wings flash in the sunlight. They are specks of beautiful wondrous color in this catastrophe of water and oil and junk. And they went to business, like they was the air force come to save us from mosquitoes. I claps my hands for them, and JayEl does the same.

On one trip, a little girl would not let go of my hand when we got to the Lady. Revel said he has to find more gasoline anyway, so JayEl and I went with the girl and her family into the Crossroads. I sat with the girl and her mother in the backyard until the girl—Maya—fell asleep.

JayEl came and sat next to me.

"I've been talking to people," he said. "It doesn't seem like anyone is coming to help. Maybe we should try and find someone in charge and tell them. Maybe they don't know how bad it is."

I nod. We don't tell anyone. We just start walking where it was dry, toward the Vieux Carre. We watch for bad people and listen for strange sounds, but we don't see hardly anyone, except some people who just climbed out of the New Sea, and they aren't looking to hurt us. We go by a store and some people carrying stuff out, mostly food stuff, some gots other things.

We get to the quarter easy enough. It so different, hardly like a storm come at all, just a day with some rain, only there was hardly anyone else around. Most the places all boarded up. They spray-painted some of the boards with messages: "Go home, Miss Thing." "Let the good times spin." "We'll be back."

"This is bizarre," JayEl said. "It's like a whole other world."

We heard the sound of music playing and followed it to an open bar. A couple people sat at the counter, drinking. The bartender saw us and waved us inside.

"What you need, dawlin'?"

"We want to call someone and let them know there are people out on rooftops and in the projects and out in the water," I said. "Thousands of them. They need help."

"Our phone doesn't work," he said. "I'm sure someone is coming to help. You want something to drink?"

"We don't have any money," JayEl said.

The bartender leaned down and came up with two bottles of Coke. He took off the caps and held the bottles out to us.

We took them.

"You sit down and rest a bit," he said.

JayEl and I sat at one of the tables. I looks around. I never been in a bar before.

"Didn't you get the hurricane here?" I asked.

"Sure we did, *cher*," he said. "We just didn't get the water. You did?"

I nodded. "We all drowned."

"I hear the water is still rising," he said. "We could all be underwater before it's over."

The men at the counter turned to look at us. They smiled.

"You been out in da water, *cher*?" one asked.

We nodded.

"You seen any mermaids?"

"We seen a lot of dead things," JayEl said. "Nothing else."

"I hear they see dolphins," one said.

The other said, "No, them alligators."

"I hope not," I said. "That water is nasty. I haven't seen anything alive in the water, at least nothing that's got to breathe underwater."

We drink our Cokes and then go out again, after giving our thanks to the bartender. We see a news crew. Some woman stands in front of a camera with a microphone.

I tap one of the men in her crew on the shoulder and say, "Is help coming? There are people all over the rooftops and in the water and everywhere."

"We're trying to tell them," the man said quietly. "Everybody thought New Orleans had missed the big one, but then a bunch of levees failed on top of the storm surge."

"So they know?" I said.

He nodded. "They know."

"Where are they?"

The man shook his head.

JayEl and I looks at each other and keeps walking.

"They came and helped those people in the tsunami right away," JayEl said, "and that was a long ways away. This is right here in the United States. They'll help us."

"It's been two days," I said. "Where do you think everybody is?"

"Maybe they're just in another part of the city," he said.

"I hope so," I said.

I takes JayEl to Miss Jenine's Mask Her Aid, just to see. The door is open. I goes inside the small store. The pretty masks still hang from hooks and nails all over everywheres. I looks for the humming-bird mask.

"Who there?" I hear Miss Jenine's voice. Then I see her coming down the little spiral staircase. She dressed in a shiny dress with a long boa. She had paint all over her face.

"Ruby! Dawlin'! How you be? You at work to-day? I went this morning, but it's closed. You bring me some beignets?"

Miss Jenine's eyes were all shiny. She gots closer and I thought she probably been drinking. Or sum-thin.

"You okay, Miss Jenine? The café is closed. Don't you remember the hurricane?"

She laughs. "That wasn't much, was it? Though I will say I was a little afraid here all by myself. Thought the whole world was shaking. But I feel fine now. I'm going down to Mickey's. You want to come? Who is this beautiful boy?"

"This is Jacob Williams, Miss Jenine," I said.

"You come with me," she said. "I'll buy you dinner and a beer."

"We need to get back," I said. "I'm glad you're okay."

"Never better," she said. "Ta, dawlins!"

She went out of her store and into the street, waving as she walked away. We stepped out and I closed the door behind us.

"Does she realize there isn't any electricity or water or plumbing?" JayEl asked.

"I don't know," I said. "I've never seen her like that."

"I think she's drunk," he said.

"Must have been scary to be all by yourself in the dark like that."

We stopped at Café Brouhaha. It was all closed up. Everything looked fine. Then we started back to the Crossroads. As we went near one store away from the quarter, we saw some men with guns and other people taking things out of the store. One of the men shot the gun. JayEl and I ran and didn't stop to see if anyone was hurt. When we got back to the Crossroads, it was almost dark. And I mean dark. No lights. The Lady had some kerosene lamps and candles lit. People huddled around each other in her backyard and in the store.

Mr. Lagniappe and Mr. Williams were there. They come up to us right away.

"Where have you been?" Mr. Williams asked. He had the full of fears look. "I thought something happened to you."

"We were out helping people get to dry land," JayEl said. "Then we walked around to see if we could get help. We didn't see any police or government people, just some news crew."

"Where's Mammaloose?" I asked, looking around.

"We came back looking for you," Mr. Lagniappe said. "We couldn't find the neighborhood."

"What do you mean?" I asked.

"We got lost," Mr. Williams said. "I was all turned around. I couldn't get my bearings. We came back to get you, but we couldn't find you. So we went back out to rescue other people."

"Oh my god," I said. "We've got to go out and get Mammaloose! She's been there all day by herself."

"Ruby," Mr. Lagniappe said, "it's too dark. We'll have to wait until morning. She'll be all right until then."

"But you both know where we live!" I said. I felt sick. I couldn't believe it. I never had a thought that they couldn't find our house!

"I'm so sorry, Ruby," Mr. Williams said. "I know this area, but now the houses and street signs and other things are gone or moved. I didn't know where I was."

"But you know where I live," I said to Mr. Lagniappe.

"I'm sorry," he said.

I looked at JayEl.

"She'll be all right," he said. "She's a tough old bird."

I started walking around in circles. "What if the water went up? What if the house collapsed?"

"The water isn't going up that much," Mr. Williams said. "She'll be all right."

"But she thought I was going to desert her, and now I have! She's all by herself. That's gonna drive her crazy."

The Lady came up to us then. She put her hand my back, and I stopped walking.

"You worried about your grandma?" she said. "It won't be nice, but she'll be okay. I knew your grandma a long time ago. She used to be involved in all kinds of community things. She was able to look after herself."

"But she was so afraid," I said. "And I was so mad at her."

I started chewing on my fingers.

"Ruby," Mr. Lagniappe said. "There's nothing we can do until morning. I'm sorry."

I'm sorry, I'm sorry. I loves you, I loves you, I loves you.

I walked away from them. I didn't go far 'cause it got dark right away once I gone from the Crossroads. JayEl followed me.

"I put angry words on her before I left," I said.

I walked in circles again.

"It's about time," he said.

"She told me that she took me from my momma and daddy," I said. "My mom was a druggie and she'd robbed a store, so Mammaloose told my daddy that he had to give her one of his daughters or she'd tell the police on my momma. So he did. And then she told me they was dead."

"Oh, man," JayEl said.

"And I do have sisters. Opal and Pearl. They're real. I didn't make them up."

"I never thought you did," JayEl said.

"*I* did," I said. When you're told your whole life that you is crazy, after a while, you is crazy. Well, Mammaloose never said I was crazy, and I never had the thoughts I was crazy, but I did wonder if I had made everything up, that maybe Mammaloose was right about everything being part of my imagine."

"Where are your sisters now?" JayEl asked. "Why didn't they come see you?"

"I don't know where they are," I said. "She said she made my daddy promise to stay away. My momma was around for a while. She lived on our block for a time. I don't know if you remember Miss Emmy?"

"That was your momma?" he said.

"What? What's wrong with that?"

"Nothing," he said. "It's just that she . . . she was wasted all the time."

"I never noticed those kinds of things back then," I said. "I just thought she was a nice woman. But my sisters are older. They could have come seen me by now. Before I left Mammaloose she made me promise to come back for her. She said she'd tell me where they were if I came back. That just pissed me off. I don't need a bribe to do the right thing."

My eyes adjusted now to the dark and I could see JayEl. He said, "We'll go first thing. You won't get lost. You know where all the Rooted People are."

"That's right," I said. "I won't get lost."

JayEl took my hand, only this time it didn't feel like when we was kids. He held on to it for a minute, and I felt funny in my stomach, kind of queasy and nice all at the same time. Then he let go.

"Let's get something to eat," he said.

We went back to the group and ate more soup and bread. People talked quietly. Some told stories of how they got caught in the storm or why they didn't leave or what they had seen. Some of them wondered how their people were doing. I listened to them and thought, I am so sorry. I loves you, I loves you, I loves you.

Maya came and held my hand again, like she did in the boat. I sat her on my lap.

She said, "I don't like the dark."

"Oh, sweetheart," I said, "you can see so many things at night that are hidden during the daylight. Look, night is the only time you can see the ashy skin of the sky."

Maya looked up.

"You see?" I asked.

Maya nodded.

"Some people call that the Milky Way," I said.

"Because it looks like milk?" she asked.

"Uh-huh. In a country called Finland, it's called the Pathway of Birds. That's because the birds follow it when they're migrating. In Hindu stories, it's called the dolphin disk. They imagined the stars are in the belly of a dolphin. What's it look like to you?"

"Like a river in the sky," she said.

"Then maybe it is," I said. "A river of stars and planets and light and darkness. But you can only see it when it's dark. And guess what?"

"What?"

"We're part of that river," I said. "Or that Pathway of Birds or the belly of a dolphin. The Earth is part of the Milky Way."

She stared at the sky. I could see her face and eyes and nose and ears as she imagined it.

"Have you ever heard anyone say 'Abracadabra'?" I asked.

"When they're playing magic," she said.

"Yep, well, some think that *abracadabra* means 'I create as I speak.' So it means we can create our world as we speak. Maybe every time we say something we are helping create our world. Like this place. It looks dark and scary to some people—and it smells bad from all the bad water. But I see it as a place where I met you and where people come to be safe and get food. Like a church. Or what they call a sanctuary. So we could name this the Lady's Sanctuary. That name puts more truth on it than just saying it's a dark and scary place."

Maya looked around. I could tell she liked that name.

"Ruby here names things all the time," JayEl said. "Like out front of our store, she calls it the Place Where I First Met JayEl. Or her bedroom—she calls that the Place Where I Dream."

"Or where the hummingbird came the other day," I said. "That's now the Hummingbird Bench. Even though it's in an old empty lot with weeds and garbage. I can look at that bench and it seems the whole place lights up because of the Hummingbird Bench."

"I'd call the boat where I was with you this morning the Ruby Boat," Maya said.

I smiled. "I like that just fine."

We went into the store and found places for the children and the sicks to sleep. It seemed every spot was eventually took up by a some ones. I talks to Mammaloose in my head. "You be all right, Mawmaw. Just hang on. We be there first thing. I'm sorry. I loves you, I loves you, I loves you." I may be mad at her, but that didn't mean nothing, really. Not when it's the end of the world.

Mr. Williams and Mr. Lagniappe put a ripped plastic garbage bag on the ground, and the four of us lay on it, trying to sleep. I could hear people whispering and crying and coughing and farting all around us. One group in the far corner of the yard sat by the lantern, trying to figure out if anyone was going to come get us.

"They just gonna let the poor people die," one man said. "That was the plan all along."

"I bet all the rich people saved," another said.

"I heard Lakeview got flooded just as bad," one woman said.

I cringed. That would mean the Home of the Big Oaks and the Flying Horses was flooded too. I could imagine the big old oak trees surrounded by water, the flying horses drowned, the bayous now lakes. My whole body hurt just thinking on it.

"They'll rebuild Lakeview," one man said, "you wait and see. They gonna bulldoze our neighborhoods, put up condos for rich people. This ain't ever gonna be home again."

"Who cares? I don't need to be drowned more than once to know I need to get outta here."

"I seen the police putting this woman in handcuffs after she come out of the store with diapers and food for her three kids. Put her right down on the ground, then argued about where to take her, while her three kids standing there crying."

"I asked the police how to get to the Superdome and they wouldn't even answer me. Like I'm nothing."

"You are nothing. You ain't got a car, you ain't got no money, you nothing in this city or in this country."

Mr. Lagniappe whispered to me, "You still awake, Ruby?"

"Uh-huh."

"You try to sleep, dawlin'. We find your grandma in the morning."

I didn't say anything. I listened to JayEl, Mr. Williams, and Mr. Lagniappe fall to sleep. Other people up, watching, guarding. I couldn't sleep. I hear the dogs. Screams in the distance. Glass breaking. A helicopter far away. Or coming near?

I gets up and find the Lady. We sit on the back steps together.

"You worried about your mawmaw?" she asked.

"Yes. She told me some things during the storm. She said my momma, daddy, and sisters all alive! My daddy give me away when I was small so that he and Momma stay out of jail."

I tell the Lady everything Mammaloose told me. She listens and nods. I had night eyes now, and I can see her. She don't seem to have any surprise on her about this.

"I knew your grandmother," the Lady said. "She was a fine woman. She was always helping her neighbors, always trying to make things better around her.

She loved your momma. I knew your momma too. We went to school together. Something happened to your momma. I don't know what. She got sad or mad. Something. And the drugs just made her a different person. She got cleaned up and met your daddy. He was a good man, but he had problems for a while. He tried to make a life for your momma and you kids out in the swamp, but it was hard. He come to the city and it took him a long time to settle down. And your momma couldn't keep off the drugs for very long. Your daddy was worried she would hurt you all or leave you alone too long. When your grandma offered to take you, your daddy was glad. Not to have you gone, but he knew you'd be safe with your grandmother."

"Why'd she have to threaten him so he'd never come around again?"

"She was desperate," the Lady said. "She was trying everything to save her daughter and grandchildren. Then she felt like she could only save you. So she held on tight."

"Do you still know my momma?"

She shook her head. "I don't know where she is, *cher*."

"Why didn't you tell me? Why didn't someone tell me?"

"This was a family thing," she said. "I wouldn't go against your family. I figured when you were eighteen, someone would tell you. I think your grandmother was going to tell you after your birthday, once you were settled in to college. I don't really know. I don't think family secrets are good, but they weren't my secrets to reveal, you know?"

I could hear rustling in the deep, dark night.

"Do you think we're safe here?" I whispered.

"I've got guards," the Lady said. "We won't get robbed tonight. But I hope the water starts going down and help comes for these people soon."

"When I was small, I named everything," I said. "You know, like the trees were Rooted People and the birds were the Flying People. I think I did that because I thought if human people could see that everything is important—everything is kin, is people

—then the world would be a better place. People could see how we all belong together, humans and trees and birds and the swamp. You know. But now I see it doesn't do much good to be any kind of people. Looks like they've just left us here to drown or rot or die."

The Lady shook her head. "*Cher*, we just got to take care of ourselves somehow. Even when this is all done. I heard once someone say that if we lose our awe in things, then everything is for sale. Maybe we lost our awe for Nature, our awe for our lives, so everything is for sale: our air, our water, our planet, each other. You, Ruby, you've always had that awe. You can see how things can be different, better. You can see the truth. Hang on to that, dawlin'."

I went back to where JayEl and his daddy and Mr. Lagniappe were. I lay down next to JayEl. He opened his eyes and looked at me. I looked at him.

"I'm sorry you came back for me," I said.

"I'm not," he said. "I'd be up in Baton Rouge wondering what was going on."

"You'd probably know more about what was

going on if you were there," I said. "Unless they got the hurricane too. Maybe the whole state got hit."

JayEl was quiet. I'd forgotten his momma was up in Baton Rouge.

"I'm sure it's okay," I said. "I'm just talking so I don't hear all those noises in the dark."

Mammaloose was up in that attic hearing the dogs and the screams and silence in the dark all by herself.

"This reminds me of us camping in our backyard when we were kids," JayEl said. "Remember? We had that little pup tent. You'd tell stories of magical swamp creatures. That good luck white alley gator. The charming and friendly armadillo."

"Ms. Army Dillo. She knew how to throw a good *fais do-do*."

"I never understood why Good Luck Alley Gator never ate anyone. And the Rooted People liked being in water all the time. Hard to believe."

"They were bayou trees," I said. "Of course they liked being in the water. My stories were better than yours. Yours were always about ghosts and ghouls and people coming back from the dead."

"That's what you do on camping trips," JayEl said. "You tell scary stories."

"Your stories were just icky," I said.

"Everyone's a critic," he said.

I laughed quietly.

"I wish Ms. Army Dillo and Good Luck Alley Gator were around now," he said.

"Yeah, me too."

"Ruby," he whispered. "Do you ever—do you ever think we could be more than friends?"

"What do you mean, more than friends? Ain't nothing more than friends. That's the best thing in the world. That will last forever. Maybe we'll be friends and something else. Is that what you're asking?"

"I'm asking if you ever think you could go crazy over me?"

I smiled. "No, JayEl. I won't go crazy over you or anyone else. You might make my stomach flutter a little bit, things like that."

"I make your stomach flutter?"

"Either that or I've just been feeling a little queasy," I said. "The end of the world and everything."

I could hear the smile in his voice. "Yeah, okay."

I held out my little finger. "Forever friends."

He linked his finger with mine. "Friends forever."

This time we didn't pull our fingers away from each other.

"You know, the sooner you go to sleep," he said, "the sooner it'll be morning."

"I don't think that follows," I said.

"Well, it'll seem sooner."

"Awright then."

I closed my eyes and fell to sleep with JayEl's finger wrapped around mine.

CHAPTER 9

Wounds Day

THE DAY began taking off night when I woke up Mr. Lagniappe. The Lady was already awake and cooking up something to eat. I ate quickly. I don't even remember what. Maya was curled up next to her momma, so I whispered a goodbye so I wouldn't wake her. Then Mr. Lagniappe, Mr. Williams, Jay-El, and I went out to the boat. The gangsters were still guarding it, and Revel's boat. I wondered if he had found gasoline for his.

The water didn't look like it was down at all. Maybe higher. And it stank even worse. Like something dead—and more some things rotting and gasoline and chemicals, and it made me gag. We set off. People on the rooftops still there. Didn't seem to have as much energy as yesterday—though even yesterday they didn't have much. Other people out on the New Sea too. People helping people. We heards helicopters.

I told Mr. Lagniappe where to take the boat. I'd point to that old oak and then Mr. Lagniappe would figure out how to get there. Then that sycamore. Another old oak. Then that tree. Or this one. Then I'd see a building I knew. Even wrecked I knew it.

It took us a much shorter time to get there than it had to row away from it, though it still too long. But finally we go past JayEl's daddy's store and then down to Mammaloose's house. It looked so strange without its roof, like some giant come down and pull off the roof and left the rest.

"Mammaloose!" I called.

I didn't see her. We got closer and I called again. I couldn't see her. Maybe she was sleeping. Maybe she couldn't hear us.

"Mammaloose!" I yelled.

Mr. Lagniappe put the boat close to the house, then they helped me up onto the porch roof—which wasn't easy. I scrambled up it and then pulled myself up and over and into the attic.

The attic was empty. Mammaloose wasn't there.

My heart started beating in my ears.

I kept calling her name. Don't know why. It was a small place, and she wasn't there.

I looked at the closed attic door.

Did she go down there?

I hesitated, and then I opened it. I had such fear to look at the water, but I did. She wasn't there.

I lean down and calls her name.

What if she went down to get something and slipped and drowned? What if she was hurt?

I let the ladder down, and then I slowly went down. I put one foot into the water and held on to the ladder until my foot touched the floor. The water went up to just below my knees. I sloshed through it, calling, "Mammaloose! Mammaloose!" I went to my room and looked around. She wasn't there. I looked at where the stairs were, now drowned in water. She could have fallen. She could be in the water.

I wanted to scream then. I wanted to wail and scream and cry.

I sloshed through the water to the ladder. I

climbed up into attic again. I felt panicky. I looked around. All I could see was desolation and ruin and water. Forever. That's all there was forever.

"Ruby!"

JayEl's voice.

I looked down.

"She's not here," I said. "Maybe she drowned."

Then I looked down at the attic floor. The bag of beignets was gone. I starts laughing. I could see Mr. Williams and JayEl and Mr. Lagniappe looking at me. They must have thought I lost my mind. But I hadn't. The bag was gone. Mammaloose must have taken the bag of beignets with her. And the bottle of water.

"She's not here," I said.

I climbed down off the house again. This time I jumped right into the arms of those three men. They caught me.

"They must have come for her," I said.

"Then she's safe," Mr. Williams said. "They would have taken her someplace where she's getting food and water. Shelter."

I nodded. "I hope so. I hope she's not all alone."

"Let's stop by the store and pick up supplies," Mr. Williams said.

Mr. Lagniappe turned the boat around.

"You feel better?" JayEl asked.

"A little," I said. "But I need to know that she's all right."

"I still don't know why you care," JayEl said.

"Jacob," Mr. Williams said.

"Do you know what she did to Ruby? She let her believe her whole family was dead or didn't exist!"

"She's still her grandmother," Mr. Williams said.

"So if Hitler was her grandfather, would that mean she should make nice with him?" JayEl asked.

"Jacob, that's not a good comparison," Mr. Williams said. "Mammaloose probably thought she was doing the right thing."

"She was wrong," Jacob said. "She was messin' with Ruby's life."

"Mammaloose isn't Hitler," I said. "She's just mixed up. And right now, she might be in trouble. That's all that matters."

We stopped by the store. JayEl and Mr. Williams went in and got canned goods and water and tossed them into the boat. Then we returned to the Lady.

Someone had gotten batteries for the radio, and we listened to the news. No body was coming. Or at least no one had come yet. Tens of thousands of people were stranded in the city—and at the Superdome. People were looting—or getting supplies to live on. Someone was shooting at rescue workers.

"Who would do that?" Mr. Williams asked as we all stood around the radio listening.

Buses were supposed to be on their way to New Orleans, but the only buses anyone had seen were drowned along with most of the city. Fires burned around the city. Newcomers to the Superdome were being locked out. Parts of the Louisiana and Mississippi coast had been obliterated. Authorities expected the death toll to be in the thousands. There was no good news. There was no bad news. There was only awful news.

I felt like I was gonna throw up again. Mr. Lagniappe put his hand on my back.

"You okay?"

I nodded.

I couldn't complain. I was one of the lucky ones. I was safe. Mammaloose was safe too. Somewhere. I hoped.

"Come on, ladies and germs," Revel said. "We got people to save. Good morning, Vietnam!"

"Lady," I said, "I've got to find my grandma."

"Where would you go, *cher*? You don't know where she is."

"Aren't they dropping people off at the Superdome? Maybe she's there."

"You can't go by yourself," the Lady said. "It's too dangerous. And we need the boats to rescue people."

"I know," I said. "I'll walk as far as I can. Maybe it's not flooded there."

"I'll take her," Mr. Lagniappe said.

"I'll go with her too," JayEl said. He looked at his daddy. "Maybe we can phone Mom from there."

I looked at the Lady.

"See, I'll be all right."

"Take some food and water," the Lady said.

"When it's all over, we'll get together and we'll have some stories to tell!" She gave me a hug.

We decided we would take Mr. Grant's boat with us. With two of us on each side, we carried it between us. We walked through the French Quarter again. We found more media people, and we asked them if they knew about all the trapped people. They said they did and that they were telling the world.

"Doesn't seem to be doing much good," JayEl said. "Nobody's coming."

We walked along the riverside, where it was dry. Seemed kind of funny that we in a flood but it ain't the river that done it. They would call this a natural disaster. I didn't see nothing natural about. I'd call this an unnatural disaster. The levees people make failing. The chemicals and gasoline people make going into the water. The swamp dried up and not able to help soak up the water. How is that natural? I reflect on all of this as we walk. None of us says much. Then we have to leave the riverside and go up toward the Superdome. There is a little water here. Mr. Lagniappe and Mr. Williams don't want JayEl and me to get in any of the water. So we walk around stuff and follow our own twisting and turning path to get to the dome without touching water. Some places we just could not avoid the water, so JayEl and I got into the boat and Mr. Lagniappe and Mr. Williams pulled it.

"I feel like I'm two years old," JayEl said.

"So what?" Mr. Williams said. "Your momma would kill me if I let you get in the water. Just think of it as saving my life."

It wasn't very high water and there was less debris here than back in our neighborhood, so it was easier to walk in for Mr. Lagniappe and Mr. Williams. Still, I worried about them. The water was filthy.

As we got near the dome, we could see people all around. I felt the glads feels just then. People! Thousands of them. We hid the boat once we were close, just in case we needed it again. Then we followed the other people headed in the same direction. The sun beat down on us. I was so hot, I felt lightheaded. As we got closer to the throngs of people, I started having the bad feels again. They all looked sick and tired and sweaty and hungry and angry and sad. There was litter everywhere, and the stink of sweat and urine and feces came toward us like a rolling fog. It wasn't worse than what we'd smelled on the water, but it was bad.

"My god," Mr. Williams said. "Why are all these people still here?"

"Do you think they've all been here since Sunday?" JayEl asked.

"I don't know," Mr. Williams answered.

"Should we split up and look for Mammaloose?" I asked. "Though Mr. Lagniappe should stay with one of us because he doesn't know Mammaloose."

"I don't think we should split up," JayEl said. "We might never find each other again."

"JayEl's right," Mr. Williams said. "Let's stay together."

This next part was hard. I never seen nothing like this in my whole life. I hope I never sees it again. We went looking for Mammaloose outside the dome first. We saw so many sad and helpless people. I remember looking at people on the TeeVee from other countries who was all drenched and scared and hungry and even though Mammaloose and I don't have lots of money I never felt like those people and I never thought we would look like those people. Now we were the same. We all the same, I guess, once we are homeless, once what we know is gone.

Most people were tired and lost, some angry and lost, a few drunk and angry. Mostly people seemed to be waiting for something and something never come.

Waiting, waiting, waiting.

And then we went inside the superdome. I never been there, so I didn't know what it was like other times. Now it was dark and so hot and humid and stinky. It was like I was breathing in sweat and crap. I had to put my shirt over my nose and mouth. And it was dark. We looked around for Mammaloose. We looked for hours. Inside and out. We saw some people we knew. Found Her Man Lionel and Miss Sweet Desserts. They hadn't seen Mammaloose.

We didn't find Mammaloose. Mr. Lagniappe and Mr. Williams talked to people while JayEl and I found a spot a little ways from everybody to sit and breathe and think. We didn't even talk. It was just too awful. Not more awful than the water. No, but out there we had been able to do something. We had helped some of those people. Not here. Nothing to do here. We couldn't take these people anywhere. I saw some guards dressed in camo or fatigues, walking around with their guns.

If trucks of soldiers could come here, where were the buses to take all these people to safety?

Mr. Williams and Mr. Lagniappe said some people told them that the Coast Guard had been setting people down on the highway. Maybe Mammaloose was up there. It was close by but hard to get to.

"You want to go up on the highway and look for her?" Mr. Lagniappe asked.

I nodded.

We walked away from the Superdome. No one paid us any attention, at least as far as I could tell. I followed Mr. Williams and Mr. Lagniappe. I wasn't sure they knew where they were going, but I followed anyway.

After a while, we were up on the highway walking toward a large group of people. They looked even more tired and bedraggled and lost than the people at the dome. One little girl was crying. She reached her hand out to me. I held out my bottle of water to her as I knelt next to her.

"How you doin', dawlin'?" I asked.

She shook her head.

"You drink that water," I said. "You feel better."

She dropped the bottle. Mr. Lagniappe leaned over and picked it up. As he did, a cord around his neck fell out of his shirt and a little white alligator hung down from it. The little girl reached for it.

"You like that?" Mr. Lagniappe asked.

She nodded.

He took it from around his neck and put it around hers.

"It's yours," he said. "It's a good luck charm."

"I never seen that on you before," I said. "I didn't know you come from the swamp."

He didn't answer. We kept walking, looking at all the faces. Seemed like everyone was asking us if we had heard anything. Are the buses coming? Is there food coming? Water? Anything?

I looked down the highway — empty except for these people and the cars left along the side — and I looked out at the city that was buried in water and I had thoughts about apocalyptic stories again — about the veil being lifted. What would be revealed now?

JayEl stood next to me as I looked around. "I don't even know what to say, seeing all this," he said.

"It's like people forgot we are part of nature," Mr. Williams said. "You cut off your arm, eventually you're gonna bleed to death."

Mr. Lagniappe said, "There's Mammaloose."

What? I thought. He don't even know her. But I looked where he was looking and there was Mammaloose sitting on the side of the road looking like one of those women I had seen in pictures about the Dust Bowl, only different.

I ran to her, my arms out. She tried to push herself up to stand, but she couldn't. So I fell on my knees and put my arms around her, and she put her arms around me. "I'm sorry!" I said. "I loves you, I loves you, I loves you." At the same time, she held me tight and said, "I'm sorry. I love you, I love you, I love you."

After a while, we let each other go. I wiped her tears and she wiped mine, and it didn't even feel funny her touching me or me touching her. It was like this was always what we were meant to be like but somehow it had never happened. I stood up and helped her to her feet.

"Mr. Lagniappe," I said, "How'd you know it was Mammaloose?"

"Ruby Marie," Mammaloose said, "this here is your daddy, Callaway Pelletier."

"Mammaloose," I said. The heat must be getting to her. "This is Mr. Lagniappe. I've told you about him."

"I know who he is," she said. "I always knew who he was. Lanier was his momma's name."

"Hello, Ruby," Mr. Lagniappe said, as though it was the first time I ever met him.

I looked over at JayEl. His mouth was open wide.

"What?" I said. "So your daughters? Are Sugar and Honey Opal and Pearl? Where are they?"

"Yep, and they're where I said they were," he said. "They had planned on coming down for your eighteenth birthday."

"Where's Momma?"

"She's in Chicago," Mr. Lagniappe said. "She's working as a secretary. She's been clean now for a little while."

I could only stare at Mr. Lagniappe.

"Daddy?"

"That's right, Ruby," he said. "I'm your daddy."

"I don't know if I should be angry or happy," I said.

"I know what I'd be," JayEl said.

"But it's what I've always imagined," I said, "having my family. It seems kind of stingy to be angry at the way I get it."

I held out my hand to Mr. Lagniappe. "It's nice to meet you again, Daddy."

Then I started crying. Before long, Mr. Lagniappe had his arms around me, and we were both crying.

We all sat down at the side of the road under the hot sun and we shared what food and water we had with each other, letting Mammaloose having the biggest share. I kept looking at Mr. Lagniappe, trying to see my daddy when I looked at him. I remembered all the times I'd watched him make the dough, knead it, punch it, roll it. I always felt comforted watching him: always reminded me of my daddy cooking.

The sun went down. From up here, we could see the fires, hear screams, gunshots, dogs, people crying, coughing, laughing, moaning. And we were out in the open, no shelter, just ourselves under the stars. It was so frightening listening to the sounds in the dark coming from the near and far distance — listening to sounds we didn't recognize. So we started telling each other stories. Other people gathered round us and joined in. I wondered if this was what it would be like for the rest of our lives. We ended up looking at the stars and pointing out which constellations we knew or didn't know. And somehow, we fell to sleep again, me and JayEl halfway curled around each other and Mammaloose and Mr. Lagniappe and Mr. Williams.

For the first time in my memory I was able to say, "Good night, Daddy," and get an answer.

"Good night, sweetheart," he said. "Sweet dreams."

CHAPTER 10

IN THE MORNING, I saw that everyone looked worse than they had the day before. JayEl and Mr. Williams and Mr. Lagniappe and Mammaloose all looked like those people we had rescued two days ago: glassy-eyed, dazed longgoners.

I stood up. Just then, a green dragonfly came right up to my face. He hovered there for a moment. Then he flew on down the highway.

"We need to leave this place," I said, looking at the rest of my apocalyptic family.

"Do you know something we don't know?" Mr. Lagniappe asked.

"Only what the Green Dragonfly told me."

"What was that?" Mammaloose asked.

"'Go north, dirty stinky treasure girl.'"

JayEl laughed. "Then let's go."

"I think she's right," Mammaloose said. "The only way we're getting out of here is on our own."

"So we're going to just walk down the highway?" Mr. Williams asked.

I nodded. "That's what the dragonfly said."

"I'm with my granddaughter," Mammaloose said. "She knows about these things."

Mr. Lagniappe nodded. "I'm with my daughter. She knows about these things."

JayEl held up his little finger. I wrapped mine around his. Then we pulled away.

"Let's go," he said.

We turned away from the city and started walking down the highway.

"You okay to do this, Mammaloose?" I asked.

"I'm not helpless," she said. "You don't worry about me."

"I'm sorry you were left by yourself," I said. "I tried coming back for you. I did come back, but you were gone."

"It did me good," she said. "I realized how alone you must have felt all these years. I should never have made your family stay away. I'm sorry I did that."

We heard a car honk. Surprised, we all turned around. A small white car stopped next to us. The driver rolled down his window.

"You need a ride?"

"Can you fit all of us?" Mr. Williams asked.

"I can take three and come back for the rest," the driver said.

"We're not getting separated again," I said. "Thank you anyway."

He drove away, and we kept walking. A few minutes later, the same car drove up again. How'd he do that? I wondered. The man stopped the car, got out, opened the door to his back seat, and pulled out two suitcases. He put them on the side of the road.

"Come on," he said. "Squeeze in. I can't leave you here."

"There are so many others who need help," I said.

"And we're some of those many," Mammaloose said. "Get in. It's what the green dragonfly said."

Mammaloose sat in the front seat. The rest of us

squeezed in to the back. I was half on JayEl's lap, half off. I didn't mind. The car lurched forward. We all giggled and laughed and made noises. Then we looked back at the city. I thought of all the others left behind. We all thought of the others.

"We're the lucky ones," Mr. Lagniappe said.

We all got quiet, and the man drove us away from the city.

CHAPTER 11

Ruby's Imagine

I'D LIKE to tell you everything turned out just fine, but it didn't. Lots of things are still up in the air months later. Things still not the same — but then, they shouldn't be.

We made it to Baton Rouge that day, safe and sound. JayEl's momma was so happy to see us. Her sister welcomed us into her home. That night I got to talk to my sisters, Opal and Pearl. I don't know that any of us said much. We cried a lot. We promised to talk to each other all the time and see each other as soon as we could. Mr. Lagniappe returned to New Orleans the next day to get the Lady, but he couldn't get back in. Buses did eventually come and take out the people at the dome and on the highway. Many families were split up and taken to different parts of the country. They call this the Katrina diaspora.

That word means "to scatter." Lots of scattering and shattering. Less than a month after the Big Spin, Hurricane Rita sent another storm surge through New Orleans, drowning again many Gardens of Neighbors.

It is months later and parts of New Orleans still looks like the day after the Big Spin, minus the water. I saw pictures of the Home of the Big Oaks and Flying Horses. It was drowned. All the places I sat and walked were gone. Later the water went down, and most of the old trees survived. The Flying Horses got damaged bad, mold and water. I'm not sure what will happen to them or to the park.

Mammaloose, Mr. Lagniappe, and I got an apartment in Baton Rouge near JayEl and his parents. It wasn't easy because none of us had any money. Eventually Mrs. Williams got a job as a teacher, and JayEl and I went to school in Baton Rouge together. Mammaloose is still looking for a job, and Mr. Williams is doing some work as a carpenter. They had hurricane and flood insurance, but they still hardly got anything. Mr. Lagniappe helped Mr. Burden re-open Café Brouhaha. He wouldn't let me go work there because he said it wasn't safe to be in New Orleans yet. He stayed there five days a week, sleeping in the back of Café Brouhaha or over at the Lady's, and came back to Baton Rouge two days a week. Yes, the Lady managed to stay in New Orleans even when they tried to make her leave, and Mr. Lagniappe finally told the Lady that he loved her. I had glad feels about that.

I spent Thanksgiving and Christmas with Mammaloose, JayEl and his family, and Opal, Pearl, and Daddy. The more I'm with my family, the more I remember. And the more I talk like everyone else, JayEl says. He misses the other way. I say I'm just learning who I am, so things are bound to change.

After the water went down, Mr. Grant was found in his house, drowned — his lady friend was there too. I felt bad I'd thought he'd made her up all that time. We still don't know what happened to Uncle Gilbert. We hear all kinds of stories. Someone said they saw him in Mississippi; someone else saw him in a shelter in Houston. Mr. Lagniappe put a note up on our door for him. Mammaloose hasn't been back and she doesn't know if she ever wants to go.

Mr. Lagniappe and I went back to Mammaloose's house a couple months after the storm. We wore masks over our mouths and noses, but it still stunk. Mold was growing over everything downstairs. I couldn't find anything we could salvage. Upstairs in my room, I took down the bird feeders from my locker. The hummingbird feeder had mold all over it, but the other bird feeder seemed fine. In the top of the locker I also found the little tin box with Opal's book inside. I took it and the feeder outside. We had brought some birdseed just in case, so we filled the feeder with it and hung it from the porch. Then I opened the tin box and looked inside. The book had escaped the mold. I opened it.

"Daddy," I said. "I found this box and book when I was small. I always thought that Opal had given it to me. Did she?"

Mr. Lagniappe looked at the book in my hand. He swallowed and blinked.

"I got that for Opal's birthday one year," he said.

"Found it at a library book sale. Fifty cents. She read it, but she didn't really understand it. She said the girl reminded her of you, so she and Pearl took turns reading it to you. You loved it. You were always talking to the trees and the birds and the wind and the clouds and naming things, like the girl Opal in the book. Just before you left us, Opal put that in the bottom of your bag. Your grandma must have saved it for you. I'm glad you still have it. You should show it to your sister."

"I will, Daddy."

Just then a sparrow flew up to the feeder. Daddy and I got very still and watched. It wasn't Samuel Beckett Sparrow. Maybe one of his friends.

I whispered, "Tell Samuel Beckett Sparrow and Maya Angelou Hummingbird I says hello."

Opal changed her wedding date to April first. Mr. Burden offered to host the wedding at his place. He closed down for the day. It was a great party. We laughed and cried and ate and danced. It almost felt like before the Big Spin came—only better.

Afterward, my family sat around the big table with JayEl and his family and Mr. Burden, who seemed much less burdened now that the storm had come and gone. They all talked about what they thought was going to happen now.

Mammaloose said, "What do you think, granddaughter?"

I looked around the table and said, "Abracadabra. I think I have the glad feels today. I think that I see miles and miles of swamp filled with alley gators and egrets and fishes and worms and bugs and Rooted People and Flying People and human people, and the ground is squishy and mushy and it can soak up a lot of water. And this city is part of it all. The air is so clean, we just want to keep breathing so we can drink it in along with everything else. Our water doesn't have a drop of chemicals in it that ain't supposed to be there, 'cause all the people here loves, loves, loves everyone else and knows we has to keep the air and water and earth clean. People rebuild the houses here to use the sun to power them. There's a whole lot of jobs created just to make these houses and cars. I can see it. Can you? All the pretty houses with panels where the sun comes down and kisses them and fills them with electricity. And there's no more poor people. Not because they goes to live somewheres else. No! Everyone has jobs they likes and cares about. They have work that inspires and heals them. They have homes of beauty. And the Home of the Big Oaks and the Flying Horses is even better than before, with green spaces all over the city so that the city itself is a green space. I can see it. I can see the parties and the food and the laughter and the love. I loves, loves, loves it. Can you see it? Can you feel it? Can you make it happen? Yes, yes, yes. This will be the Place Where We Renewed the World." I tapped my chest. "Right here." I looked around. "Right in all of us. At least, that's what the Old Oaks told me."

"That's Ruby's imagine!" JayEl said.

I laughed.

Everyone at the table clapped.

"Now! More dancing," Mr. Burden said.

I danced with my daddy and my sisters. I showed JayEl how to dance too.

Later, I went to the back and found my daddy making bread.

"Whatcha doin', Daddy?"

"Helps with stress," he said.

"Stress," I said, standing next to him. "What stress you got?"

He looked at me. I laughed.

"I'll make you some café au lait," I said. "It'll make you forget your daughters are all growing up."

He pulled on the ball of dough, folded it over, pushed it down, folded it again. "I'm sorry about the way you had to grow up. I'm sorry I wasn't there."

"You were there," I said. "I just didn't know it. It's all water under the bridge. It's a flood under the bridge!"

He smiled. "Maybe we'll get your momma to come to your graduation."

"Maybe," I said. "That would be fine."

The Lady came into the back. "There you are,

dawlin'. Come on back to the party. Your married daughter wants a dance."

"I'll finish this," I said.

Mr. Lagniappe washed his hands. He kissed me on the forehead. The Lady winked at me, and then they left together. JayEl came into the room.

"So this is where you used to make those delicious beignets," he said.

"It is," I said. "But those days long gone."

He stood next to me. We looked at each other and then we kissed.

He smiled. "So now you can call this the Place Where JayEl First Kissed Ruby."

I laughed. "For one thing, you didn't kiss me, I kissed you. Or we kissed each other. For another thing, there already is the Place Where JayEl First Kissed Ruby."

"What are you talking about?"

"Out back of your house by the oak tree. That's the place. We were about eight. You kissed me and asked if I would be your girlfriend. I said not if you did that again."

JayEl laughed. "I don't remember that! How could I have forgotten?"

"You were probably so devastated by my rejection," I said.

"Probably."

He held up his little finger.

"Friends forever," he said.

I curled my finger around his.

"Forever friends."

Author's Note

LIKE MILLIONS of other people all over the world, I watched television as Hurricane Katrina approached the Louisiana coast in August of 2005. I was afraid the devastation would be unimaginable. And then the hurricane hit. At first, we thought the city of New Orleans had been spared. Phew! Once again the city below sea level had made it through another storm. But we were wrong. And it only got worse when the levees broke and the water rose. The storm left, but the water stayed.

We watched for days as the storm victims waited for help. I remember wondering why the news people could get into New Orleans yet the government couldn't seem to get there and help anyone. We saw exhausted, stunned people trapped on their rooftops, on the tops of their cars, on their balconies. I wanted to help them. I remember yelling at the television:

"Someone do something!" I called my congressman and senators; I called the president. But that was about all I could do besides donate money. If I was so frustrated and upset, I could only imagine how terrible it was for the people still down there, still waiting for help.

Almost as soon as I learned about the hurricane, I saw a group of Hurricane Katrina survivors in my mind's eye coming together to help one another after the storm. My coping skills involve my imagination. I couldn't help the people in New Orleans, but I could write a story. Ruby came to me speaking her own special dialect—the dialect of a child of the world—and I wrote her story as though she were telling it to me.

Ruby reminded me of Opal Whiteley, a girl who lived in the Pacific Northwest in the early part of the twentieth century. Opal had an uncommon connection to nature and a unique way of speaking and writing. She believed in fairies and talked to the trees, the creeks, the animals. (Something I did as a child too. Well, actually, I still do it.) She and Ruby would have been kindred spirits, no doubt. When my best friend Linda Ford was ill, I sat by her bed and read her passages from *Opal*, a compilation of Opal's diaries. Opal brought my friend great comfort. I promised Linda that one day I would write a book that honored her and Opal. I hope that *Ruby's Imagine* does that.

I've always had a soft spot for Louisiana. I made my entrance into the world on a humid March morning not far from the Red Chute Bayou and the Red River, inside a hospital on Barksdale Air Force Base in Bossier City, Louisiana, where my father was stationed. Although I cam screaming into this world amid stainless steel and concrete, I like to think my first breath sucked swamp gas and Voodoo dust into my baby lungs. As I watched the Katrina survivors all those years later, I knew I could have been one of them. Any of us could have been.

I wanted to write Ruby's story to honor the people of Louisiana and Mississippi who went through Hurricane Katrina and its aftermath too. I hope it helps in some small measure for them to know they haven't been forgotten.